# APRIL'S
# WITCHES

# APRIL'S WITCHES

by
BEVERLY CROOK

Steck-Vaughn Company
An Intext Publisher
Austin, Texas

To
Compton

# CHAPTER

# I

The Hiland hills are hie, hie hills,
The Hiland hills are hie;
They are no like the banks o' Tay,
Or bonny town o' Dundee.

*Old Scottish Ballad*

APRIL MACKENZIE FOUGHT BACK the tears as she stared through the frost-etched window of the train station. Outside was a gloomy world of leaden skies and swirling snow. Inside was the empty station; even the stationmaster had left.

"Maybe they don't want me," she whispered. The thought had been with her since her arrival, and it was almost a relief to say it. Yet it frightened her. "I'm being silly," she told herself quickly. "After all, I'm family!"

The word "family" held little comfort because it stirred up painful memories. She might as well

1

face it; she had no family, not since the boating accident that had taken the lives of her mother and father. Since then she had discovered that gangling, teen-age girls without money or parents were a surplus commodity. There simply wasn't any demand for them.

If she needed further proof, she had only to remember the past seven months with her uncle and his family. Uncle John, her mother's brother, had done his best to make her feel welcome; but the odds were against him. Cousin Tina, at thirteen, wanted to keep her bedroom a private world and resented sharing it with an intruder. The eight-year-old twins, on the blacklist of every baby-sitter for miles, felt honor bound to eliminate the threat of a "built-in" sitter. And Aunt Sara, while loudly proclaiming martyrdom for taking in an orphan, complained just as loudly about the extra work and expense involved. So it had been with relief all around that arrangements were finally completed for her to live with Elsbeth and Millicent Mac-Kenzie, her only other living relatives.

It would be different this time, April was sure. For one thing the MacKenzies were rich, and she wouldn't be a financial burden to them. And more importantly, they wanted her; they had insisted that she come. But where were they now? Why didn't they put an end to this suspense?

2

She looked out the window again. The snow had drawn an opaque curtain across the landscape; nothing was visible. She sank down on one of the station's hard benches, suddenly aware how tired she was. The long trip from California to this remote spot in the mountains of western Maryland had left her bone-weary. But she couldn't relax—not yet. There were too many uncertainties keeping her on edge.

If only she knew her aunts, that would help, but she had never met them; and her father had seldom spoken of his family in Maryland. All she knew was that both aunts were unmarried and that they still lived in the great, stone house her grandfather had built here in Glen Ayr. Her father had mentioned that house occasionally, how it stood high above the town and how it had been the talk of the countryside when it was built. Her grandfather had called it Greystone, but everyone else called it the Castle.

Her spirits lifted a little as she contemplated life in a castle. At least she would have no money problems, which was fortunate, considering the small amount of cash in her purse. After the lawyers had written up all those long papers with the fancy seals and everyone had been paid, there was almost nothing left.

It wasn't her father's fault, though, no matter

3

what Aunt Sara said. He couldn't help it if he loved spending money, despite his Scottish ancestry. It was a natural reaction to his own father's stinginess. She remembered that sometimes her mother had been angry because he bought things they couldn't afford—like the boat, for instance. But no one could stay angry with her father very long. They had kept the boat, and sailing had become their favorite hobby until . . . until that day her parents had gone sailing while she was in school and a sudden storm had come up. But she wasn't going to think about that anymore. It was time to start looking ahead.

A loud stamping outside the station door interrupted her thoughts. Her heart skipped a beat. "They're here at last!" April found herself exclaiming.

The door burst open, but only the little stationmaster came in. He looked at her in surprise. "Thought you'd be gone by now. You're Mrs. Andrews's granddaughter, aren't you?"

"No, I'm going to the MacKenzies. I'm their niece."

The gray-haired man stopped shaking snow from his coat and looked at her with new interest. "You mean the MacKenzies on the hill? You're their niece?"

She didn't know why this news should be so hard

4

to swallow, but apparently he was having trouble with it.

"Maybe they didn't get the telegram about when I was coming, or they can't get through the snow . . ."

The stationmaster clucked sympathetically, and she felt the tears well up again.

"Don't you fret! We'll get you there," he assured her. "Telegram office is in the general store; and with the holidays coming and all, probably no one's fetched it up the hill. As soon as I bank the fire, we'll see about getting you there."

He lifted the lid on the potbellied stove and poked at the fire. "Rufus Roberts is the name. What's yours, lass?"

"April. April MacKenzie."

He cocked his head to one side. "So you're Jim MacKenzie's daughter. Well, well! I knew your father. I was sorry to hear about the accident." He replaced the stove lid and adjusted the damper.

April wondered how he had heard about the accident. But, of course, her aunts must have told him.

As if he had read her thoughts, Mr. Roberts smiled and said, "Not many secrets in this town. A bit of news in a telegram spreads faster than a brush fire. Everybody thinks telegrams are public property."

He began tidying up the station. "No more trains coming through today," he announced. "We don't get many visitors up here in winter, except for the holidays."

He chatted on, but she was aware that he was studying her. "You going to be visiting here a spell?" he asked, trying unsuccessfully to disguise his interest.

"I—I'm going to live here," she told him uncertainly.

The old man knocked over the poker, then fumbled about picking it up. "You're going to live with the MacKenzies?" he repeated, as if he hadn't heard her correctly.

She nodded and he stared openly. Then, in an effort to cover his breach of manners, he began bustling about the station.

"I'm all ready, and Old Nell's just outside. Come along with you!" he cried with false heartiness and ushered her out the door.

At the railing of the station porch was a horse and sleigh, complete with bells. It looked just like a Christmas card picture.

"Are we going to ride in it?" April asked in delight.

"Only safe way to travel these roads when the snow gets bad," Mr. Roberts replied. "Old Nell likes the sleigh, too. Makes her feel useful again."

He helped April into the vehicle and tossed a blanket across her lap.

"Yes, sir! Best tonic in the world for old age is to feel useful," he philosophized as he stowed her luggage in the sleigh and climbed in beside her. He slapped the reins, and they began to move over the white ground.

When they reached the hard-packed snow of the road, the horse picked up speed, and they glided smoothly into the town. Snow was still falling thickly, but she caught glimpses of the picturesque houses tucked away in this mountain valley. What a quaint place! she thought. Living here was going to be fun after all.

The stationmaster cleared his throat. "You sure it's the MacKenzie place you want?"

The question was innocent enough, but April felt uneasy. Why should a visit to the MacKenzies be so unusual? Maybe he was just surprised that two old ladies were adopting a teen-ager. That must be it.

"If it's where Miss Elsbeth MacKenzie and her sister, Miss Millicent MacKenzie, live, then that's the place," April said. "I tried to call them from the station, but couldn't find their names in the telephone book. I guess they have an unlisted number."

He gave her a sidelong glance. "They don't have

a phone up there." Then he added as an after-thought, "Don't really need one, I guess."

April was surprised. No phone? And with all their money! They must be eccentric. Wealthy people sometimes got that way, she had heard.

Mr. Roberts pulled on the reins, and Old Nell slowed to a walk and finally stopped before a neat, yellow clapboard house.

"Ought to tell my missus where I'm going. She's apt to worry. Come in and have a cup of hot chocolate to warm you up a mite." He helped April out of the sleigh. "My missus makes the best hot chocolate in these parts."

He led the way into a tidy parlor with white lace curtains at the windows. In the adjoining dining room, April could see two women sitting at a table, busily talking and sipping from cups. They turned as she and the stationmaster entered; and one of them, a short, gray-haired woman, hurried forward.

"This is April MacKenzie, Jim's daughter," Mr. Roberts said. "This is the missus."

Mrs. Roberts appeared slightly stunned, but quickly recovered. "What a nice surprise! We were very fond of your father." Then, remembering her other guest, she introduced her.

"This is Mrs. MacDonald."

"How do you do?" April said, looking into a sallow face topped by obviously dyed red hair. Mrs.

8

MacDonald smiled at her, but it was without warmth; and April had the distinct feeling that although they had just met, the woman disliked her intensely.

"Sit right down," said Mrs. Roberts in a motherly fashion as she placed another cup on the table. "You must be half-frozen riding around in that sleigh. Take off your coat, that's it. Now, have some nice, hot chocolate. We'll be having supper in a bit. You'll stay, won't you?"

April was touched by her hospitality. She had felt unwanted for so long, it was good to receive a sincere invitation to linger. And although this home was quite modest, even poor by her California standards, its owners showed no hesitancy about sharing a meal.

"We'd be glad to have you stay the night, and I'll take you up on the hill tomorrow," Mr. Roberts offered.

"Thank you, thank you very much," April said. "But I'd like to get to my aunts' house before dark—if it isn't too much trouble. Or maybe I could get a cab."

The three of them laughed heartily as Mr. Roberts explained, "Old Murdock has the only cab, but you'd never get him to go up that hill!" He stopped abruptly, muttering something about the cab couldn't get through the snow.

"I'll take you myself," he assured her, but she

could sense a slight reluctance. "She's going to live at the Castle," he told the women.

"Live there!" they chorused, then stopped. The embarrassing silence that followed ended with all three talking at once.

Mrs. MacDonald's nasal voice quickly dominated. "It's ridiculous! You really shouldn't be going up there at all, my dear. Your aunts . . . well, they just can't take the proper care of you. The whole thing's preposterous!"

"Now, now, Della," Mrs. Roberts interposed. "She's their niece, and they have every right to have her if she wants to go."

"That's just it!" Mrs. MacDonald cried triumphantly. "If she wants to go! She may think she wants to go now, but if she knew anything about the Castle, she wouldn't be in any hurry to get there, you can be sure of that! It's our duty to tell her what she'll be getting into. I, for one, wouldn't be able to sleep a wink, knowing that I'd let her walk right into the devil's backyard without so much as a warning!"

Mrs. Roberts looked imploringly at Mr. Roberts. "Now hold on, Della!" he said. "There's no need to worry the girl. Seems she's had enough trouble lately. Her aunts may have their little 'peculiarisms', but they're fine people, and they'll do right by her. If she doesn't want to stay up there, she can always come back here; and I'll see that she gets a train to California."

Mrs. MacDonald sniffed. "Well, if anything happens, it won't be on my head. You'll have to live with it on your conscience."

She turned her weasel-like face to April and said in warning tones, "Some very strange things go on at the Castle. And your aunts are a little strange, too." She cast a glance at the Robertses. "I'm not trying to frighten you," she added quickly. "I'm just telling you for your own good so you'll be on your guard. No point walking on a cliff blindfolded when you could just as easily look where you're going. So don't expect things to be normal up there; then you won't be scared out of your skin." She sat back, looking satisfied.

April had no idea what Mrs. MacDonald was talking about. The only thing clear was her feeling of dislike for the woman. April was beginning to believe Mrs. MacDonald was the sort who would enjoy giving out bad news, a typical busybody.

Mr. Roberts stood up. "We'd better get you on your way. With the snow and all, it'll be dark early; and that road up the hill is tricky."

April was anxious to start, also. What Mr. Roberts called a hill looked suspiciously like a mountain on which she would prefer to travel in daylight.

She had just said good-bye, when there was a loud knock at the door; and almost immediately, a large woman barged into the room like an armored tank. She was already in the middle of a sentence: "... just for a minute, but I wanted to tell you about some plans for the Daft Days."

A boy, quite handsome and athletic looking, came in behind her and stood by quietly.

When the woman paused for breath, Mr. Roberts introduced her. She was Mrs. Ramsay, the mayor's wife, and the boy was her son, Bobby.

While the Robertses and their older guests edged toward the dining room with their heads together in muted conversation, the boy turned to April.

"Welcome to Glen Ayr," he said and nodded toward the other room. "You've made their day. Nothing new has happened around here since Mrs. Murdock had twins last month. You've given them a whole new topic of conversation."

She looked at his fair hair and blue eyes and decided he was the best-looking boy she had ever seen.

"Are you visiting here for the holidays?" he asked.

"I'm going to live here. Up on the hill with my aunts."

Bobby stared at her for a moment, then said, "Well! You've really given them something to

12

talk about!" He studied her again. "We seldom see a new face—and an attractive new one's really rare. I hope you like it here and ... and stick around."

April felt a warm ripple of pleasure at his compliment, although "attractive" was stretching a point. She wasn't ugly, but she wasn't likely to win any beauty contests, either. Her nose tilted too much, her hair was too red, and she had too many freckles. But she was grateful someone had noticed her face, for a change, instead of her height. It wasn't that she was so tall, actually. People just got that impression because she seemed to be all arms and legs.

"The high school crowd around here shows up at Thompson's drugstore most afternoons. If you stop by tomorrow, I'll introduce you—so you'll know some of the inmates when school starts again in January."

She laughed. "Thanks. That'll be a big help. New schools always scare me a little."

"I wouldn't know about that. I've never been to school anywhere but over at Clear Creek. That's the school for this district. Guess I'd feel lost in a new place, too." He shifted his feet and after a minute said, "Don't you—uh—do you like it up on the hill?"

"I haven't been there yet," April answered and

had the feeling that wasn't the question he had intended to ask.

The meeting in the dining room broke up, and Mr. Roberts joined her. April said good-bye again and climbed into the sleigh as the three women watched in uneasy silence.

"See you at Thompson's," Bobby called.

Old Nell gave a snort, tossed her head a few times as if to dislodge the cobwebs, then began a brisk trot.

As the sleigh glided down the road, the high-pitched voice of Mrs. MacDonald drifted after them: "I declare! A body never knows what's going to happen next at Witches' Castle."

# CHAPTER

# 2

When I have a saxpence under my thum,
   Then I'll get credit in ilka town:
But ay when I'm poor they bid me gae by;
   O! poverty parts good company!
                    *Early Scottish Song*

Mr. Roberts slapped the reins and startled
Old Nell with a loud "giddap!" But he was too late.
Mrs. MacDonald's words had carried distinctly
on the brittle, cold air.

"Don't pay her no mind," he said. "She lets her
imagination get out of hand sometimes."

April hadn't paid any attention, because her
thoughts were still on the handsome Bobby Ramsay. But now that Mr. Roberts mentioned it, she

15

wondered aloud, "What did she mean by saying 'Witches' Castle'?"

"Well, some folks call it that because the Castle's gloomy and ghostly. Della MacDonald thinks there's an evil spell on it, but that doesn't mean anything."

They both fell silent while the sleigh glided the length of the town, its bells jingling in time to Nell's footwork. The thick, fluffy snowflakes had dwindled to a fine confetti, and she could see brightly colored houses along the main street and nestled against the mountain foothills. They looked for all the world like toy houses sitting on white cotton in a Christmas scene. April sensed a snugness about the little community that was reassuring. It would be nice to live where everyone knew all his neighbors. She had never liked the aloofness of the big, sprawling developments in California.

Soon they had passed the last house and turned off the main road into a narrow lane. Here the fresh snow showed no sign of previous travelers. On either side, as far as she could see, were trees, mostly evergreens, all burdened with thick, white robes of snow. It reminded her of some lines of poetry she had learned once upon a time:

"Every pine and fir and hemlock
Wore ermine too dear for an earl,

And the poorest twig on the elm-tree
Was ridged inch deep with pearl."

She couldn't remember the rest of it.

Despite the beautiful scenery, the words "Witches' Castle" kept haunting her thoughts. "Why does Mrs. MacDonald think there's something evil about the Castle?" she asked.

Mr. Roberts glanced at her, then back at the road, as if making up his mind about something. "Well, Della's never had a good word about the place since she worked there. She helped out in the kitchen and around the house when your granddaddy was still alive. About that time, Miss Elsbeth had a gentleman friend named Jock Cameron. The story was that Della took a powerful liking to him, but he was devoted to Miss Elsbeth—wanted to marry her and she wanted to marry him."

"But I didn't think either one of my aunts ever married."

"Never did," said the stationmaster, "but it wasn't their fault. Sam MacKenzie had the idea that nobody was good enough for his daughters, and he suspected everyone of wanting to marry them for his money. He kept a mighty close watch on the girls and discouraged any suitors. In those days, children didn't run off and do as they pleased—not girls, anyway. It just wasn't done. So the two girls waited, and first thing you know, they weren't young anymore."

"But what happened to Mr. Cameron?"

"Well, I hear he died suddenly. Don't know if it's true or not. Anyway, when Sam MacKenzie saw that things were getting pretty serious between them, he wouldn't allow Jock to set foot at the Castle. So Jock and Miss Elsbeth took to meeting secretly at the mine, and someone found out about it and told her father. Then he fired Jock."

"Mr. Cameron was working for my grand-father?"

"Sure was. He was a miner just like most every-body in these parts, and he worked in the Mac-Kenzie mine. Old Sam was rich and powerful in those days, and no one would risk getting on the bad side of him by giving Jock a job. There's never been much to do around here except mine, any-how. Jock left town to find another job and never came back—and Miss Elsbeth never married any-body else."

"What about my Aunt Millicent? Did she have a broken romance, too?"

"I don't know about that. She did have a lot of gentleman callers at one time, but they didn't hang around long; her father saw to that. Old Sam was a mighty hard man in some ways. Of course, he only wanted to protect his daughters—probably didn't intend to give them a rough time."

The road wound back and forth through the trees until April was sure Mr. Roberts had lost his way. But Old Nell plodded on, the sleigh bells jingling nervously in the icy air.

Suddenly two great stone pillars loomed up on the left side of the road. Mr. Roberts pulled one rein sharply and guided the horse between them.

"Won't be long now. This is the driveway," he said.

The top of one pillar had fallen into a pile by the road, and the other one had loose stones that were ready to fall.

"I guess a truck or something ran into those," April said, motioning toward the entrance.

"Nope, they just fell. Should have had some cement work done on them long ago. They used to be right pretty—fanciest entranceway you ever saw."

"Why doesn't someone repair them?" April asked, puzzled that anything as imposing as a castle would have such a shoddy entrance.

"No money for repairs," Mr. Roberts replied matter-of-factly as he brushed snow from the blanket. Shrubs crowded the driveway until there was barely room for the sleigh to pass, and every disturbed branch protested with a flurry of snowflakes.

"No money!" April cried, certain that she had misunderstood.

"That's right," said the old man, settling back in the seat. "Sam MacKenzie was rich at one time—no doubt about that. But after he died, the ladies were very hard up. No money left. Some folks think there's plenty and they won't spend it, but I don't believe that. Your granddaddy was mighty peculiar in his old age. He probably let money get away from him. The ladies do have a tiny income from a trust fund their mother set up for them; but aside from that, they're as poor as church mice."

April felt physically ill, as if someone had hit her in the stomach. "Do you mean my aunts don't have *any* money?" she asked.

Mr. Roberts glanced at her stricken face. "You didn't know that?"

She shook her head.

"Me and my tongue! I wouldn't have broken it to you so suddenly if I'd thought you didn't know. My! My! I *am* sorry. But don't you worry. They get along fine. Raise food in their garden and have plenty of wood for heat. They don't ask help from anybody. They just don't have money to keep things the way they used to be, that's all."

April tried to recover her poise and felt ashamed that Mr. Roberts had seen her disappointment. But it wasn't the money she cared about, except as a welcome guarantee; she didn't want to be a financial burden again. Now she wasn't sure her aunts really wanted her. Maybe they had been pressured into offering her a home. Suddenly she felt very much alone.

Mr. Roberts tightened the reins, and Old Nell came to a halt. "Look there!" he cried, pointing toward the top of the mountain.

April looked up and, through the branches of a pine tree, saw a massive gray structure towering into the sullen sky. It was a castle straight out of the Middle Ages, as if a faulty time machine had set it on this mountain by mistake. Maryland was such an unlikely place for a castle!

April turned to Mr. Roberts. "It's just like in storybooks! A *real* castle!"

The stationmaster laughed. "Your granddaddy modeled it after a castle in Scotland where he grew up. Most everybody in Glen Ayr's from Scotland, or just a generation or two away. Came over to work in the coal mines. Of course, I'm not from Scotland—was born and raised right here in Maryland, but I married a Scottish lass, so I figure that makes me a member of the clan."

April was more interested in the Castle than Mr. Roberts's ancestry. "Why did he build *that* instead of a regular house?"

"Just an idea he had, and believe me, it surprised everybody. Old Sam was mighty close with his money; never spent a cent that wasn't absolutely necessary. But he decided to bring a bit of Scotland to this country—kind of a memorial to his birthplace. So he built this castle, and for once, he was extravagant. He always said it was worth it, though."

Mr. Roberts chuckled. "I guess it made him feel like a king, because that's the way he started acting. Don't wish to speak ill of the dead, rest his soul!" he hastily added.

April continued to look up in awe at the somber building. "It has towers at each corner!" she said, still not quite believing what she saw.

"Sure has. And Sam gave them all names. Two towers are named for rivers in Scotland, the Tweed and the Clyde, and two for rivers around here, the Savage and the Potomac. But I don't know which is which."

While they watched, a large, black bird flew from a pinnacle on one of the towers, circled overhead three times, and returned to its perch. It filled April with a strange foreboding.

The little stationmaster quickly slapped the reins. "It'll be dark soon. I won't be able to find my way back if I don't hurry."

They drove on, and April tried to get used to the idea that there was no money at the Castle, thinking that perhaps she had misunderstood. She hesitated to bring up the subject again, but finally said, "My father told me that Grandfather Mac-Kenzie had lots of money—from coal discovered on his property."

"Aye, and so he did—have money, that is. But none of it has been in evidence for many a year now. The ladies manage to make ends meet, and that's all."

April sighed. That's what she thought he'd said in the first place. Now she knew she should never have listened to a fortune-teller!

Last year at a fair, a gypsy had read her fortune in a soggy clump of tea leaves. "You are going on a long trip, and a dark stranger will bring a great change into your life," the gypsy had told her, then stopped and puzzled over the tea leaves, turning the cup around several times. Finally she had shrugged and said, "This stranger seems to have gold dripping from his hands." It was such a ridiculous fortune, April had burst out laughing, much to the gypsy's annoyance.

Ridiculous or not, she had remembered the prediction, and now she was provoked with herself for even halfway believing such nonsense. It only made the truth harder to accept.

The sleigh zigged and zagged around some sharp turns, and, unexpectedly, the trees and shrubs came to an abrupt end. Ahead a series of oval terraces, one on top of the other and each a little smaller than the one below. Perched on the highest one, like the decoration on a giant layer cake, was the Castle.

April stared at this unbelievable sight. Never in her wildest dreams had she envisioned anything like it. Her father had told her about the place, but his description had been far too conservative. He grew up here and probably never realized the impact this medieval monster had on those viewing it for the first time.

The sky turned a darker gray and large, feathery snowflakes began falling again. Mr. Roberts handed down her luggage and prepared to leave. She found his presence comforting and wished he would stay a little longer.

"It's awfully quiet. Do you think anyone is at home?"

"Oh, they're home," he said positively. "They're always home."

"Don't you want to wait until morning to leave? I'm sure my aunts wouldn't mind."

"Thank you, lass, but I promised my missus I'd be back before dark. Mind you, now, come by for a visit soon. And if you decide not to stay, I'll see you safely on a train."

Before April could thank him, Old Nell and the sleigh had whirled around and departed in a white cloud of snow. She stood watching them out of sight, reluctant to face the great, brooding structure again.

At last she turned back; the Castle was still there. She had thought for a moment it might be a mirage. But not only was it there, it seemed to be growing taller and more uninviting every second. An air of decay and neglect hung over everything.

April shuddered involuntarily as the gray sky and the gray stones combined to form a completely desolate picture. She was glad that she had waited until the twenty-sixth to leave California. Christmas at Aunt Sara's had been bad enough, but it would have been unbearable here. She looked down at the dark and silent forest on the mountainside. The valley was far below. She was completely isolated up here, almost at the end of the world. If she vanished, no one would ever know what had happened to her.

As April stooped to pick up her suitcases, a tall, thin figure emerged from the shadow of a large marble urn—almost beside her. She stood quite still, afraid to move. It was a boy with a stocking cap pulled down over his ears and a heavy, wool scarf wrapped around his neck. All she could see clearly were his eyes. They were very dark and seemed to look right through her.

How long he had been standing there watching

her, she had no idea, but he must have seen the doubt and uncertainty on her face because he said quietly, "You'll be all right."

Then he picked up her cases and set an erratic course up the terrace steps to avoid the loose and broken stones, while April attempted to follow him. He stopped before the huge castle door in an elaborate stone archway and pulled back a metal knocker in the shape of a mailed fist. April examined the odd decoration, then turned to thank him for assisting her. He had been standing beside her the second before, but now he was gone—vanished.

She shook her head. "I wonder if I'll wake up and find this whole thing is a bad dream?"

As she spoke, an odd, croaking noise sounded overhead. She looked up in time to see a big, black bird take to the air. It soared effortlessly over the Castle, before starting a downward plunge—taking direct aim at her!

# CHAPTER

# 3

Will ye come up to my castle
  With me and take your dine?
And ye shall eat the gude white bread,
  And drink the claret wine.
                    *Old Scottish Ballad*

APRIL GASPED, too terrified to move. It happened so fast and unexpectedly, there wasn't time to think. The bird continued its downward flight and before she could recover her wits, it had landed on one of the large lanterns hung on either side of the entrance.

"Car-r-runk! Car-r-runk!" it said in a gravelly voice, peering down at her from atop the lantern.

April peered back. "You ought to be ashamed of yourself! Diving at people like that! You scared me silly." The bird tilted his head and stared at her with black, shining eyes.

"Boy! You sure are big!" she said. "I guess you're a crow, only not a very neat one. Your throat feathers are all straggly." She looked around. "If anyone heard me talking to a bird, they'd think I'd slipped a cog; but in this weird place, it seems natural."

The bird showed no inclination to attack so she turned her attention back to the door. There still was no sound from within. Mr. Roberts had been certain someone was home, but what if he were wrong? What if she had to spend the night here in the snow? She gave the knocker a hearty pull. It banged so loudly, the bird jumped and added a piercing "pr-r-ruck!" to the din.

"They must have heard that down in the valley," April said. "If no one comes now, I'll try another door. There seem to be plenty of them."

A thin line of light appeared around the door at that moment, and a faint rustle was heard from the other side. April waited, relieved yet apprehensive. In this creepy setting, anything could happen. Count Dracula himself might open the door!

There was a rattle of locks and chains, and the door creaked open a few inches. April felt as if she were watching a horror movie on the late show.

Suddenly, a pile of wispy, white hair popped around the door, followed by a pair of eyes.

They stared questioningly until she said, "I'm April MacKenzie."

With that, the door was jerked wide open, revealing a plump little woman holding a kerosene lamp.

"My stars, child! Come in! Come in! Why those lawyers and your uncle all said they'd let us know when you were coming, and we haven't heard a word! A body just can't depend on anything nowadays—least of all people."

While the woman chattered, April glanced past her into the Castle. All she could see was a forbidding darkness. As she picked up her suitcases, the black bird swooped down again; and April was sure it went inside. The old lady seemed unconcerned, so April decided it must have darted into one of the recesses in the ornate archway.

"Come in! Come in!" the woman called again, and April reluctantly entered. "I'm your Aunt Milly," she said and held the lamp high to study April.

"Well!" she said at last. "You don't look much like your father, but you're a MacKenzie, I can tell that. Too bad your grandfather never knew you. Have you had your supper?"

Her sentences ran together disconcertingly, but

29

April did catch the word *supper* and realized she was hungry. Lunch had been a long time ago—another lifetime, it seemed.

Without waiting for an answer, her aunt turned and led the way into the gloomy interior. April followed cautiously. She could see little by the dim glow of the kerosene lamp, but she knew this was unlike any house she had seen, or even heard about.

They headed for the back of the place where a light flickered—a fire burning in the kitchen fireplace. April was stiff with cold, and its cheerful warmth drew her like a magnet. Halfway into the kitchen, she stopped in her tracks. There stretched out on the hearth was a striped animal. It could be a small tiger, she thought, or the biggest cat she had ever seen. As soon as it saw her, it leaped to its feet, arched its back, and hissed fiercely.

"Now, now, Genevieve," Aunt Milly remonstrated. "This is April and she belongs here, so you needn't bother with all the dramatics.

"A show-off," her aunt confided in a low voice. "She really wouldn't hurt a fly."

April was unconvinced. Genevieve was a vicious-looking specimen, and the fact that she spared flies wasn't proof she would do the same with people. The cat looked April over, then stretched and yawned and went back to sleep. April relaxed, too.

"Would you like some scrapple?" Aunt Milly

asked. "Andy brought it to us. We don't have pigs, you know. Couldn't possibly butcher anyone we know!"

April wasn't sure what this conversation was all about. She had never heard of Andy, nor had she ever tasted scrapple, but she hoped it was more appetizing than its name.

Apparently Aunt Milly never expected answers to her questions. She was already putting a big, black frying pan on a rack in the fireplace. Then she opened a window and extracted a package from a box hooked to the windowsill.

"Nature's own refrigerator," she explained. "And very economical. Now sit right down at the table and rest yourself."

Aunt Milly began cutting slices from a loaf of gray-looking pudding. She plopped the slices into the frying pan, where they sizzled and sputtered.

Without warning, a strange, rasping sound ripped through the room. April jumped so violently, she almost fell from her chair.

"That's Mr. Watson," Aunt Milly said casually without even looking up. "We call him that because he looks like a bookkeeper Papa used to have."

High on the wall opposite her, April saw two bright, yellow eyes staring from the shadows. As her own eyes adjusted to the darkness, she could make out a round head and short, little body; it was an owl! But it couldn't be real; it was too tiny! Must be a decoration left over from Halloween, she thought. As she watched, the head actually moved. It swiveled around and seemed to make a complete turn, and the large eyes continued to stare. She could see now that they looked bigger than they were because of the rings of white feathers surrounding them. The rest of the small creature was a reddish brown.

"He's one of our friends," Aunt Milly said, waving a fork in the direction of the bird. "Andy found him when he was a baby and half-starved. Andy says he's a saw-whet—one of the smallest owls around—and he's called that because he sometimes sounds like a file on a saw. Andy knows everything about animals, especially birds."

She opened a door just off the kitchen and called, "Come away, Mr. Watson! Into the cellar with you!"

There was a slight flutter of wings, then with lightning speed, the owl zoomed silently from his perch and through the open door. April breathed a sigh of relief when she heard the door click shut.

"Best mouser we've ever had," Aunt Milly whispered. "Better even than Genevieve. She's getting lazy in her old age." She glanced around to be sure the cat hadn't overheard her remarks.

April liked excitement and hated dull routine,

but for once, she'd had enough of the unusual. She wanted nothing so much as a conventional meal and place to sleep, but she was doubtful that she would find either here.

After turning the scrapple in the pan, Aunt Milly uncovered an earthenware crock sitting on the floor in a corner of the kitchen. "Josephine's fresh again," she announced and ladled milk from the crock.

There must be a cow here somewhere, April concluded and looked around warily, thinking she probably would find it in the guest room.

Finally the meal was ready, and her aunt placed before her crisp, brown scrapple; homemade bread and jam; and a glass of the richest milk April had ever tasted. Everything was delicious. For a little while, she forgot her strange surroundings and enjoyed the food.

Aunt Milly poured herself a cup of hot milk and sat at the table opposite her. "My, it's good to have you with us! We get a little lonely at times. Of course we have all our friends," she hastened to add, then stared wistfully into the fire. "We missed your father so much when he left. James was our baby brother—almost like a son to us, really, because Elsbeth and I were in our late teens when he was born. Then after Mama died, we looked after him."

April saw an opportunity to ask a question she

had put to her father, but never received a very satisfactory answer. "Why didn't Dad come back here? He almost never talked about Maryland; and for a long time, I didn't know I had relatives here."

Aunt Milly toyed with her cup and seemed agitated. "It's a little hard to explain," she said, "but sometimes when people are too much alike, they don't get along well. Papa was very headstrong, and James was just like him. Neither would give an inch. Papa had expected him to take over the mine. James was his only son; and all the men in the family have been miners for generations, first in Scotland, then in this country. But your father had other ideas. He was like Mama, always reading books. He wanted to go to college and stay as far from the mines as possible.

"Papa told him he wouldn't pay a cent for his education, so your father left and worked his way through college. He wrote to us and came back for a visit now and then, but after he started teaching in California, we didn't see much of him. California's so far away . . ." Her voice trailed off as she looked at her thoughts in the fire.

April shifted position and waited. She didn't think Aunt Milly had told the whole story.

"When was the last time you saw my father?"

Her aunt hesitated. "Well, it was some time ago.

34

Papa was getting on in years, and he'd get some queer ideas. Nothing would change his mind once he'd decided something. The last time James was here, they had a quarrel, a bad one; and your father left. He kept in touch with Elsbeth and me, but he never came here again. It was a shame! Things could have been so different."

Before April could find out more about this quarrel, her aunt called sharply, "Genevieve! Your tail's almost in the fire!"

The big cat switched its tail without bothering to move anything else.

"Elsbeth will be delighted to find you here," Aunt Milly went on, changing the subject. "She's in bed now—she isn't too strong, you know—so it might be well if you waited until morning to see her. Besides, you must be very tired after your long trip. And to think we didn't meet you! It was kind of Mr. Roberts to look after you. We must thank him sometime. He used to visit here, but we never see much of him anymore."

She bustled about, putting things away and setting the kitchen in order. When everything was arranged to her satisfaction, Aunt Milly lit another kerosene lamp and handed it to April. "I'll show you to your room now."

She picked up a suitcase with her free hand and April picked up another. Genevieve got up, stretched, and went to the head of the little procession as it moved from the kitchen to the dark hall and up the great, winding stairs. April kept close behind her aunt. No wonder people called this "Witches' Castle"! It was the scariest place imaginable—no lights, creatures popping in and out. And the noises! There was a constant creaking and rustling in the shadows—unseen things just beyond range of the lamplight.

On the second floor, Aunt Milly opened a door halfway down the corridor and ushered her into a large bedroom filled with massive furniture, including a big four-poster bed. April shivered as the cold dampness of the room penetrated her clothing.

"Hurry and get into bed before you catch your death," her aunt said worriedly. "If I had known you were coming, I'd have laid a fire." She waved toward the big, empty fireplace. "I have some nice applewood all split."

Aunt Milly turned down the bed and patted the feather mattress that had been fluffed into a great mound. Then she unfolded a down comforter. "This will keep you snug, and I have something else."

She darted across the hall and came back with a hot brick wrapped in a towel. She tucked it under the covers at the foot of the bed. "Put your feet against that," she directed, "and it will keep you warm as toast. Now, sleep well!"

She and Genevieve turned to go, but at the door, she paused. "Don't let anything you might hear bother you," she said. "The wind makes strange sounds up here, and some of our night friends stir about. Pleasant dreams!"

April stared at the closed door. "Night friends," she whispered to herself, "I wonder who they are?" Well, she couldn't check around to find out now. Her teeth were chattering, and the room felt like the Arctic Circle. There was one consolation: Any "night friends" lurking about would be chunks of ice by morning, so there was no need to worry about them. She tossed her clothes on a chair and jumped into bed.

The feather mattress was like a cloud, and she sank down into its depths. She was so tired, even a bed of nails would have felt good. As she dozed off, there was a loud thump outside the door. April sat up and listened, but heard nothing more. Just when she had convinced herself her imagination was playing tricks, there was another noise, creaking this time.

Shivers ran up her spine as she got out of bed, felt her way to the door, and opened it a crack. At the end of the dark corridor, she saw a light—from a lamp held by a tall, thin woman in a white robe.

She was carrying one end of a small, gold table, and Aunt Milly was carrying the other end. As they began to descend the stairs, a black bird swooped over their heads and gave a loud croak that resounded throughout the Castle.

Trembling with fear and cold, April shut the door. "What have I stumbled into?" she whispered.

# CHAPTER

# 4

The birds sit chittering in the thorn,
  A' day they fare but sparely;
And lang's the night frae e'en to morn—
  I'm sure it's winter fairly.
                                *Robert Burns*

APRIL RAN BACK to bed and pulled the covers over her head. Behaving like an ostrich wouldn't help, she knew; but it was the only action she could think of. As she lay there shaking, common sense began to assert itself. No use pushing the panic button just yet, she decided. There must be a reason for all this. And while Aunt Milly had seemed rather peculiar, she was probably harmless.

The important thing was to stay awake—just in case. "You must not sleep," she kept repeating as her eyelids grew heavy. "Keep calm and stay awake. You must not..."

April sat up and blinked in the bright sunlight streaming through the tall, narrow windows of the bedroom. She glanced around to find that all the menacing shadows of the night had vanished, and the room looked cheerful.

A fire was blazing on the hearth; Aunt Milly's work, no doubt. And she hadn't even heard her come in! She refused to think about other visitors who might have come in while she was asleep.

In spite of the fire, the room was chilly, but much more comfortable than it had been last night. April poured icy water from a beautiful china pitcher into a large matching bowl on the washstand. She splashed some water on her face, dried it quickly, then dressed. She wasn't looking forward to a bath under these primitive conditions.

Before leaving her room, she opened the door and glanced cautiously up and down the corridor to be sure her aunt's "night friends" weren't about. All seemed quiet, so she started toward the stairs. From a window at the end of the long corridor, she could see for miles. The countryside was neatly wrapped in snow and tied with ice—a glistening world of white, far removed from this mountain-top. Up here, she seemed to be on another planet.

40

April had seen little of the Castle's interior upon arrival. The dim glow of the kerosene lamp had distorted more than it had revealed. And it certainly hadn't shown that the place was a jungle! There were plants everywhere—climbing, sprawling, dangling. They were stuck on stands in corners, along the stone window ledges, suspended from the walls, and even on the floor.

At the foot of the stairs, a tall, dignified woman was busy watering some of the myriad pots. It was the same woman she had seen in the white robe, moving furniture.

The woman turned and watched April descend. "So you're James's daughter," she said finally. "Millicent told me you were here. I'm so glad. I'm your Aunt Elsbeth, but I suppose you guessed that." She paused. "I do hope you slept well."

April noted an uneasiness in this aunt's manner, just as she had sensed that something was bothering Aunt Milly. Maybe they were having second thoughts about having her on their hands, she thought. They weren't exactly young anymore.

With an effort, she told her aunt, "I slept fine—and late. I guess I was tired."

"No wonder, after such a long trip," Aunt Elsbeth said sympathetically. "Come, have some breakfast. Millicent will fix it if she's back. She's the cook in the family—at least for food."

Before April could figure out that remark, her

41

aunt put down the watering can and started toward the kitchen. They went past the great hall, which looked even larger than it had last night, and just as eerie. The huge wooden beams of its high, vaulted ceiling were lacy with dust and cobwebs, as were the stone ornaments at the base of each beam. Her glance rested on one ornament. It wasn't stone—it was a bird! It looked like the same black bird that had dived at her when she arrived. She recognized its shaggy throat and the curved, heavy-looking beak.

"Aunt Elsbeth!" she called. "There's a big crow up there! I think he flew in here yesterday when I came."

Her aunt came back and looked up at the beam. "Why, that's Mad," she said calmly. "You'll insult him if you call him a crow; he's a raven. Beautiful, isn't he?"

"That's his name? Mad?"

Aunt Elsbeth laughed lightly. "That's Andy's little joke. He found him—I can't remember when; time seems to run together nowadays. The bird was in bad shape. Something had caught him; but he was still full of spirit, wanted to fight anyone who came near. So Andy called him 'Raven Mad.' He gave him to us, and Millicent nursed him back to health. After he was well, he just stayed on; and now he's one of our friends."

"Oh," was all April could find to say. She wasn't used to animals because her family had never kept them. Her father had liked to leave on trips at a moment's notice and didn't want to be hampered by pets. She would simply never get used to these creatures.

April kept a wary eye on the raven as she retreated to the kitchen where Aunt Milly was coming in the back door.

"Good-morning, my dear!" she said, stamping snow from her feet. "My, it's beautiful out there! Sit down and I'll fix you some breakfast." Her attempt at cheerfulness soon collapsed, and she turned a worried face to her sister.

"I'm afraid Josephine isn't at all well. Her knee is swollen again, and she won't stand up to let me milk her. We must do something!"

"Oh, dear!" said Aunt Elsbeth. "I used the last of the ointment on Raffles's sore foot. I can make more, but it will take awhile."

"Well, do hurry!" Aunt Milly urged as she cooked scrapple and eggs for April and ladled milk out of the half-empty crock. "Josephine gives so much milk, we can't let her go too long without milking her," she explained. Both aunts seemed more concerned with making Josephine comfortable than with sustaining their milk supply.

April ate her tasty breakfast and washed the

dishes in hot water from a cauldron on the hearth. She had no idea when her aunts had eaten. Apparently they had been up for hours.

"Anything I can do to help?" April asked Aunt Elsbeth, who was on her knees in front of a large cabinet, sorting bunches of dried grasses and jars of grimy-looking roots.

"Thank you," said her aunt. "I'll need some wood. This has to be brewed outside because the smell is pretty strong. There's some firewood on the back stoop, but it won't be enough, so I'll appreciate it if you'll fetch some from the woodpile. Millicent will show you where it is."

Aunt Milly paused in her task of tearing an old sheet into strips. "We'll have to wrap you up first, or you'll catch your death of cold," she said. "The weather's very nippy this morning, and California clothes aren't much use in this climate."

She disappeared into a closet and reappeared carrying a heavy jacket, high boots, and a man's cap with earmuffs. "These should do very nicely. They're not the latest fashion, but they are warm," she said as she helped April struggle into the cumbersome clothing that reeked of mothballs.

"If you can't find any cut wood under the snow, just split a few of the logs in the shed," her aunt told her.

The snow was up to her knees, and every step

in the big boots was an effort. April began feeling very sorry for herself. Her aunts were hardly what she had expected.

Gloomily she followed in Aunt Milly's tracks down the slope to the delapidated stone building they called a barn, then worked her way through drifted snow to the woodshed. Beyond the shed and over a low fence, flocks of noisy birds were swarming around a small platform atop a pole.

Curious, she pushed on to the fence, and from there she could see the cause of all the winged excitement. The platform was covered with grain, and birds of many sizes and colors were trying to get a meal. Then she noticed the wire cages strung out below the feeder. They were set up on chunks of wood to keep them above the snow and were literally bouncing with fluttering captives.

"Who'd want to catch those little birds?" she asked aloud and immediately, dark suspicion raised its ugly head. "They wouldn't!" she told herself. "Or would they? Maybe scrapple's made from birds." The thought made her sick, then angry.

"Here's one batch of birds that won't be eaten!" she cried, indignation mounting. She climbed over the fence and plowed through the snow to the cages.

At her approach, the birds deserted the platform and flew to the surrounding trees where they scolded her for interrupting their meal. She fumbled with the door of a large cage, sending the imprisoned birds into a frenzy. Even after she opened the door, her presence kept them inside.

"You'll be next on the menu if you don't leave!" she told them; and as she moved on, they swarmed out. The next cage had many compartments with a separate door for each. She could see that the doors were activated by little treadles. When a bird entered the trap and touched the treadle, the door slid down behind it.

"Very ingenious! But I'll have you free in a jiffy."

She had raised all but one door, when an angry voice beside her asked, "And just what do you think you're doing?"

April jumped. She had neither heard nor seen anyone approach, yet there, standing firmly astride in the snow, was a pair of heavy boots. Her gaze traveled up to the face of their owner—none other than the mysterious boy who had carried her suitcases when she arrived. It was uncanny the way he appeared and disappeared, as if he weren't quite real. She pretended to ignore him, hoping that he would go away again.

"I said, why are you meddling with those traps?" he repeated, this time a bit more loudly.

Apparently he couldn't be ignored. April stood

up, but even then had to tilt her head to see his face, or the portion that was visible. He still wore the stocking cap pulled down around his ears and a scarf that seemed to April a mile long, wound around his neck.

"I'm not meddling!" she said defiantly. "I'm turning these poor birds loose. If you're responsible for trapping them, you ought to be ashamed of yourself! Besides, you're trespassing."

For a moment, April thought she saw a twinkle in his dark eyes, but his reply belied it. "See that fence you climbed over?" He pointed to her telltale tracks in the snow. "That's the beginning of my property. *You* are trespassing! And interfering with these traps is a federal offense, so in the future, don't bother them!"

April looked at him in astonishment. "But . . . but the MacKenzies own all this land." She waved her arms to take in the whole mountain.

"Only on the other side of that fence," he said positively. With that settled, he knelt in the snow beside the only trap that now held a bird. From a leather bag slung over his shoulder, he removed a piece of bright-colored knitting yarn on which tiny silver bands were strung. He slid off a band and spread the ends apart with a pair of pointed pliers.

April watched him reach into the cage, deftly

47

gather the little bird in his left hand, and remove it from the trap. Holding its head between his first two fingers, he extended the toothpick leg and slipped the band on it. Then he swiftly squeezed the ends of the band together with the pliers and twirled it to test its fit.

"White-throated sparrow," he said and held the bird out for her to see.

April had never been so close to a wild bird before, and its coloring surprised her. At a distance, it had seemed dull, but now she could see the distinctive white throat that gave it its name, the black and white stripes on its head, and a bright, yellow spot by its eyes. It was a striking little thing.

The boy slowly opened his hand, but the bird lay limp on his palm and made no attempt to fly.

"It's dead!" she whispered in anguish.

"Playing possum," the boy replied and waved his hand. Sounding a harsh "chink!", the bird flew into a fir tree where it alternately "chinked" and pecked at its band. Finally it whistled two high, clear notes, followed by a series of wavering ones.

"Some folks call it the Peabody Bird because it seems to be saying, 'Old Sam Peabody Peabody Peabody!' " The boy imitated the rhythm of the bird's call perfectly.

April was fascinated. "The band won't hurt its leg, will it?" she asked, but got no answer. The boy was gone.

She looked in every direction; there was no sign of him. "He's done it again! It isn't possible, yet he does it. He's definitely not for real!"

She turned toward the shed and remembered her errand. "Good heavens, the wood! And Aunt Elsbeth's waiting for it! That boy's enough to make me forget my head!"

She hurried back over the fence and to the shed. Most of the cut wood was buried in the snow, but by scratching around she was able to find enough to fill her basket. She was relieved that she wouldn't have to chop any this time. She had never handled an axe before. "Probably cut my foot off," she muttered.

As April left the shed, she glanced back and saw that the birds had returned to the platform. Next time he materializes, I'll ask why he bands them, she thought. But I'm glad he turns them loose instead of serving them up in a pie or something.

She felt a little conscience-stricken for having suspected her aunts of setting the traps. Still, it was the sort of thing they might do. They weren't exactly run-of-the-mill aunts.

April trudged through the snow, dragging her heavy basket of wood. As she approached the Castle, that somber pile of stones glowered down at her. Sunlight wasn't the right setting for it, she thought. It should always be shrouded in mist and thunderstorms.

Then she saw, silhouetted against the bright sky, the tall, thin form of Aunt Elsbeth. From the steaming cauldron beside her, blue ribbons of smoke curled upward, followed by pink vapor that swirled into grotesque shapes as it danced with the wind. From high on the Castle wall, a soot-colored bird croaked and took flight, soaring lazily over the tableau beneath him.

The wind wailed, and April was certain she heard a shrill voice crying, "A body never knows what's going to happen next at Witches' Castle!"

# CHAPTER
# 5

O who will shoe my bonny foot?
    And who will glove my hand?
And who will bind my slender waist
    Wi' a broad and lilly band?
                *Old Scottish Ballad*

JOSEPHINE MOANED, and the MacKenzie sisters
hovered over her, applying a very foul-smelling
ointment to her swollen joint. While Aunt Milly
bandaged it with clean muslin, April plopped down
on a bale of hay. Right now she would have pre-
ferred being in the kitchen; but with Mr. Watson
perched there making his peculiar noises, Mad flap-
ping around, and Genevieve looking hungry, the
barn seemed the lesser risk.

"There! That should do it!" Aunt Milly announced. "I declare, Elsbeth, I don't know how we'd get along without your medicines."

She turned to April. "When Mama was alive, an old woman who lived over in the Fergusson woods used to come in and help with the cleaning—Aunt Elvira, we called her. She was a real magician with herbs, had a cure for everything. She took a liking to Elsbeth and taught her most of her secrets. And Elsbeth was a good pupil," she said proudly.

"I'm afraid I'll never be in a class with Elvira," Aunt Elsbeth replied with a modest smile. "Her most special secrets went with her to the grave because she never wrote any of them down. She couldn't write."

Josephine had stopped complaining, and the two aunts fussed about her stall, rearranging the straw and packing up their medicines. April stretched out on the hay and closed her eyes, thinking that she would have to be careful to stay well or she might have to sample her aunts' "medicine." And the cure could be worse than the disease.

As she relaxed on the hay, a sharp pain stabbed the back of one hand. April yelped and sat up suddenly, only to stare into the beady eyes of the smallest rooster she had ever seen. He glared belligerently and appeared ready to attack again. Her aunts rushed over just in time.

"Gabriel! You behave yourself!" Aunt Milly cried. "You really are naughty sometimes!" She shooed the rooster away to a safe distance.

Aunt Elsbeth examined the small cut on April's hand. "A little of this ointment I brewed for Josephine will fix it up fine," she said.

"Oh, no! It doesn't hurt at all!" April protested, preferring to suffer a dozen pecks rather than the smell of that ointment.

"I'm sorry he frightened you," Aunt Milly apologized. "Gabriel doesn't mean any harm. He just doesn't like strangers. Now that he knows you're part of the family, he won't bother you again."

April had strong doubts about that. The rooster was still glaring at her and ruffling his iridescent feathers.

Aunt Milly looked at him admiringly. "He's a spunky little thing. Keeps a sharp lookout for intruders, just like a watchdog."

"You mean you have trouble with burglars—way up here?" April asked.

"Well, not really burglars, but someone . . ." Aunt Elsbeth coughed discreetly, and Aunt Milly plunged into an account of Gabriel and the tax man.

"I know it wasn't kind to be amused," Aunt Milly confessed, trying to look repentant, "but he was so rude to us! He came to reassess the property and wanted to snoop into things that didn't concern him at all. So it did my heart good to see that big, overbearing man being chased by that tiny rooster." She threw back her head and laughed gaily. "He never did come back!"

"Andy gave Gabriel to us," Aunt Elsbeth volunteered. "I'm surprised he hasn't been around this morning. He usually stops by after he checks his bird traps."

"Bird traps?" April asked dully as the identity of Andy registered. Up to now she had assumed that the "Andy" her aunts regarded as an authority on everything was a middle-aged man, certainly not a boy only a little older than herself.

"Does he wear a cap pulled down over his ears and a brown jacket?" she asked.

"Oh, you've seen him!" Aunt Milly cried in surprise.

"I think so. I saw a boy at some traps near the woodshed." She was reluctant to give any details of that encounter.

"Did he have a striped scarf around his neck?"
April nodded.

"Then that was Andy Fergusson. We knitted the scarf for him, and he wears it *all* the time."

April found it reassuring to know she hadn't imagined this character, but it didn't make him less mysterious.

"Why does he band birds?" she asked. "I mean, what's the point of it?"

She seemed to have touched on a favorite subject because both aunts wanted to tell her about Andy's activities. As usual, Aunt Milly deferred to the more authoritative Elsbeth.

"That's how they find out all about birds," she began. "Where they migrate, what their habits are, and everything. The Fish and Wildlife Service in Washington—I think that's what it's called—has people all over the country banding birds and sending in reports. Then when a bird with a band is trapped or found dead, that's reported, too. Eventually, when the Service gets enough reports together on one kind of bird, they can get a pretty good picture of its life history."

"It's really very interesting," Aunt Milly chimed in. "Andy explained it all to us, so we put out bird feeders and made some little water pools all around to attract more birds. And we've been learning to identify them."

"Last summer one of Andy's fox sparrows was trapped by a man in Newfoundland," Aunt Elsbeth added. "Can you imagine? A little creature like that flying so far!"

April agreed that it was interesting, but it still didn't tell her much about the boy himself or why he pretended to own part of this mountain.

"Does he own land beyond the shed?" she asked casually.

"Not really," Aunt Elsbeth said as they left the barn and started back to the Castle.

So *he* was the one trespassing! April thought. She felt vindicated until Aunt Milly spoke.

"He rents that land from us. You see, his farm adjoins our land down on the slope. His people owned it before Papa bought the rest of the mountain. I remember Papa used to get so mad because the Fergussons wouldn't sell out to him. After Andy's mother died—his father was already dead, killed in a mine accident—he moved back here with his grandmother. Now Andy runs the farm."

"He's a bonny lad!" Aunt Milly declared as if he needed defending. "He's not had an easy life, but he's a bonny lad!"

He might be "bonny" to her aunts, but April found him definitely odd.

They entered a rear door of the Castle and went into the kitchen where the giant cat still slept on the hearth. Strange sounds that April tried to ignore came from various parts of the room.

Aunt Milly took off her hat, and her cotton-candy hair stood out in all directions. She poked at the fire, then bustled about preparing dinner. April still thought of the midday meal as "lunch" and found the idea of a heavy meal at noon depressing. But that didn't prevent her from eating heartily.

Aunt Milly ladled up bowls of thick, hot stew, and it was delicious. April was glad she didn't know what was in it.

"This will put some meat on your bones, April," Aunt Milly said.

Aunt Elsbeth studied her critically. "You're much too thin, but we'll have you rounded out in no time."

April knew she should appreciate their concern, but all she could think of was the story of "Hansel and Gretel"—and how Hansel had been fattened up. She wished she could stop being so suspicious of these two.

As they ate, April decided that it might be a good time to broach the subject of a trip to town. She was eager to see Bobby and to be with other young people again.

"Would you mind if I went into Glen Ayr this afternoon?" she asked. "Bobby Ramsay promised to introduce me to some of my future classmates, and I thought it would be fun to meet them."

"Go into town!" they chorused. Aunt Milly looked dismayed, and Aunt Elsbeth's lips tightened into a thin line. April had thought her aunts might consider it discourteous for her to take off so soon after arriving, but she was unprepared for outright disapproval. She wondered if they would actually forbid her to go.

"It really is a long walk, especially through all this snow," Aunt Milly began.

Aunt Elsbeth said nothing, but her lips tightened even more. A ball of cold fear swelled in the pit of April's stomach. Surely they weren't planning to make her a prisoner here?

At last Aunt Elsbeth spoke, not to April, but to her sister. "I think, Millicent, that we'll just have to accept the situation and hope for the best."

April didn't have the faintest idea what she was talking about, but her aunts must have reached some sort of decision, and Aunt Elsbeth attempted an explanation.

"We don't mind your going into town. It's just that we weren't expecting you to go right away. You surprised us, that's all." She smiled to make light of the past few moments. "Have a good time, but do come back early. The road down the mountain can be very treacherous."

"I won't stay long," April promised. Then, on impulse, she asked, "Would you like to come along?"

Her aunts looked startled; then both began talking at once.

"Oh, my!" cried Aunt Milly.

"Dear me!" said Aunt Elsbeth. She quickly recovered her composure and went on, "Not this time. We—we don't often go into Glen Ayr."

"It's a long way," Aunt Milly said again, "and Andy is good enough to shop for us if we really need anything. Of course, we used to go into town quite often when we were younger—drove a beautiful pair of horses then."

"And lots of people visited here," Aunt Elsbeth said, with a faraway look in her eyes. "Especially for Hogmanay. Why, come to think of it, the Daft Days are almost here! We'll have to start planning our Yule dinner."

"Oh, my, yes!" Aunt Milly agreed. "We celebrate Hogmanay quietly now, but they still make a big to-do in town. Maybe some first-footers will stop by this year," she said a little wistfully.

April looked blank. She was beginning to think her aunts spoke a different language. "First-footers and Daft Days?" she questioned.

Both aunts looked at her in surprise. "You mean you didn't celebrate Hogmanay in California?" Aunt Milly exclaimed. "And you a MacKenzie!"

"I'm afraid not," she said. "But we did have Yule dinner—on Christmas Day."

Her aunts shook their heads at this astonishing news. "Well, your father probably just went along with the customs of California," Aunt Elsbeth rationalized. "But it's hard to believe a true Scotsman wouldn't have longed for the Daft Days."

"Most everyone in Glen Ayr's Scottish, you

know," Aunt Milly explained. "They, or their fore-fathers, brought the holiday over with them—just as it's been celebrated in Scotland for centuries. It's a wonderful, gay time!"

"Is it the same as our New Year's Eve celebration?" April wanted to know.

"Well, Hogmanay comes at the same time," Aunt Elsbeth told her. "It used to mean just the Eve, but now some folks lump both the Eve and the Day together and call them *Hogmanay*. They're also the Daft Days or Crazy Days, been called that since olden times. It's the one time of the year when Scotsmen go a little mad. And there are parties and visiting and little children going around begging for cakes."

"Oh, we used to do it when we were little!" Aunt Milly chirped. "Remember, Elsbeth? 'Hogmanay, trollolay, Hogmanay, trollolay,'" she chanted. "Everyone would give us oat cakes."

Her sister smiled as she reflected on happier times. "And do you remember this?

'Rise up, gude-wife, and shake your feathers,
Dinna think that we are beggars;
We are bairns come to play,
And to seek our Hogmanay.'"

She recited the old lines with a thick Scottish accent that came as a surprise to April.

What a pair these aunts were! And what would

they dream up next? Probably no one had heard about this holiday for centuries, and here they were still celebrating it. Every day was a daft day at the Castle, that was for sure!

April sat on a bench in the great hall to pull on the clumsy boots her aunts had resurrected and to put on the heavy jacket, while her aunts hovered over her, helping to extricate her from all the vines and greenery.

"There certainly are a lot of plants here," April said, positive this was the understatement of the year.

Her aunts looked pleased. "Elsbeth always did have a way with growing things," Aunt Milly said with pride. "Probably because she has a green thumb."

"Millicent will have her little joke," said Aunt Elsbeth, self-consciously tucking her left hand in her apron pocket.

But not before April had seen it. Her thumb really was *green!*

# CHAPTER
# 6

The hunter now has left the moor,
The scatter'd coveys meet secure;
While here I wander, prest with care,
Along the lonely banks of Ayr.
*Robert Burns*

THE SNOW LAY DEEP on the road; and April
slogged determinedly through it, still in shock over
Aunt Elsbeth's colorful thumb. She had had no
chance to ask questions about it, because her aunt
had sailed off to the kitchen, obviously in a slight
huff over Aunt Milly's disclosure. It was just one
more unexplainable thing in an unexplainable
house.

The heavy boots made traveling slow, and April
resolved to buy a new pair, and maybe a hat, as
soon as she reached a store. She had very little cash
left, but she did have one valuable asset: her moth-

er's diamond-set wedding band. If things got really desperate, she could borrow money on it.

After what seemed an interminable length of time, the little picture-postcard village didn't look a bit closer. She considered going straight down the mountain, "as the crow flies," instead of following the winding road, but decided against it. There could be fallen trees and all sorts of obstacles hidden under the snow, and the slope was very steep. Yet someone had been brave enough to walk there. She could see footprints coming up the slope and going back down the road—probably Andy's. He seemed to turn up everywhere.

She glanced back toward the Castle, half expecting to see the black bird circling in the sky, but there was no sign of it. Not seeing the bird was as bad as seeing it, she decided. When it was visible, she could at least keep an eye on it.

April pushed on, her spirits falling as she contemplated her sad lot. Castles were rapidly losing enchantment for her.

"One of these days I'll get married and have a home of my own," she said aloud. "A completely normal home." Then she was struck by a depressing thought: who'd even ask her for a date if he had to brave snow and ferocious animals to get to her house?

Her melancholy thoughts were abruptly cut off by a chopping sound that rang through the forest.

63

She had been vaguely aware of the noise for some time, but now it was close by. After rounding a hairpin curve in the road, she saw a sleigh and someone loading trees into it. The tree cutter had his back to her, and she was about to duck out of sight when he turned. It was Bobby Ramsay!

He hesitated, as if uncertain whether she had seen him.

"Hi! Bobby," she called and ended his doubt.

He came toward her, wearing a sheepish grin. "Hello, April. Had no idea you were wandering around here."

He offered no explanation of his presence, although April felt sure he was trespassing. This land belonged to either the MacKenzies or Fergussons, she thought, but probably everyone helped themselves to the trees. After all, there were enough of them.

When she made no mention of the trees, Bobby seemed to relax and become as charming as he had been the day before.

"If you're going into town, my chariot awaits." He gave a low bow, then brought the horse and sleigh back to the road and helped her in.

He was one of the few boys with whom she had immediately felt at ease. With his good looks and pleasant personality, he was probably the most popular boy in the high school.

"I was wondering if you were going to descend

from Mount Olympus and visit us mortals down below," he said as they started toward town, the cut pines piled high behind them.

April laughed. "Too bad there isn't train service from Mount Olympus. It's an awfully long walk!"

"That's the price you pay for mingling with the gods. By the way, how do you like life in a castle? Is the place full of ghosts and goblins and bats?" She had the impression he was only half-joking.

"Oh, yes! They're all over the place," she replied. "Haven't you ever visited there?"

"Not exactly," he said and paused. "Your aunts don't want company, I'm afraid."

This was news to her. She thought her aunts loved company, but that the long, treacherous road limited visiting during the winter.

"Why do you say that?"

"Well, for one thing, they keep all those wild animals around, ready to attack anyone who gets within range. There's even a skunk—complete with perfume. That isn't the same as a welcome mat, you know."

For someone who had never visited the Castle, he seemed well informed about it, but she hadn't met any skunks as yet.

"My aunts have this thing about animals," April said. "They like anything that creeps or flies. But they don't mean to scare people away."

"Well, they've scared just about everyone who's

65

been there. Mr. James, the tax assessor, is still talking about the monster that attacked him. Says it was some sort of reptile with feathers. And your aunts didn't do a thing to help—just laughed!"

April couldn't resist a smile. "They told me about that. It wasn't a reptile; it was only Gabriel, a bantam rooster. He can't do anything but peck."

Bobby looked skeptical. "Maybe your aunts didn't tell you the whole story. After all, some very strange things go on up there; and if you knew all about them, you might not want to stay."

Bobby was echoing her own thoughts. The Castle was an odd place, and there were a great many things she didn't understand.

He glanced at her and seemed to sense her misgivings. "If you ever need any help or want any problems solved, just come to old Uncle Bobby." He exaggerated a grin, and she couldn't help giggling. What fun it was to be with him! And he was sympathetic, too. She felt he really was sincere about wanting to help her, and she needed to tell someone about her doubts and fears. But it was too late to confide in him today. They had reached Glen Ayr.

There was a sense of timelessness about the little town, as if someone had forgotten to wind it up about fifty years ago and it had lain unnoticed in the world's vest pocket ever since. The past and present were all one here.

Main Street was fairly wide, with all the businesses concentrated along it. Other streets, narrower and more winding, left Main and ran off into the foothills. A few cars and trucks made their precarious way over the hard-packed snow, but the horse-drawn sleighs outnumbered them. There had been no attempt to clear the snow from the streets, April noted—possibly because it snowed so often.

"There's Thompson's up ahead," Bobby said, pointing to a nondescript-looking store. He turned to her. "I'll buy you the best milkshake in Maryland—maybe in California, too."

April realized she was still wearing the heavy boots and funny-looking cap her aunts had provided. But Bobby didn't seem to notice, so it wouldn't matter what anyone else thought about them. She clambered out of the sleigh while Bobby tied the horse to a metal ring set in the curb.

Inside, the drugstore looked like a movie set for an oldtime ice-cream parlor. It must not have changed since the day it was built. Mostly young people were present, sitting at the tables or lounging about talking and reading the store's magazines. As April had suspected, Bobby was very popular. His athletic prowess had made him something of

67

a local hero, and everyone stopped to greet him. He acknowledged the greetings with the easy banter born of long acquaintance, then introduced her. It wasn't really necessary, though, because they seemed to know all about her. And she detected a slight coolness in their reception.

To April's surprise, everyone was preoccupied with plans for Hogmanay. Her aunts hadn't been talking about ancient history after all. Judging from what she heard, this was the biggest event of the year.

"You arrived just in time for a braw Hogmanay!" Bobby stated. It was taken for granted that anyone able to walk would be on hand for the celebration.

"I haven't any invitation," she protested. "I can't just barge in on a party."

Bobby laughed heartily as they joined a group at a large, circular table. "You don't need an invitation to Hogmanay," he explained. "Everybody has open house; and the whole world can come, even perfect strangers."

"But you mustn't be a first-footer," warned a round-faced girl named Betty. "If a woman, especially if she has red hair like yours, enters a house first on the Eve, the family will have bad luck all year."

The others nodded solemnly. "I'm not much luck, either," said Bobby, "because I'm blonde. But if I carry a lump of coal, at least I'm no disaster. Now Lot here," he indicated the thin, bespectacled boy sitting across from her, "is a great first-footer. His hair's as black as the coal in the mines."

Although the boy was right in front of her, this was the first time April had noticed him. He was one of those people who simply blend into the background. Lot smiled at her and drew his small frame up an inch or two.

April thought at first they were teasing her. Then she realized they were deadly serious about these superstitions, which were genuine beliefs, not to be taken lightly.

Bobby ordered the milkshake he had been touting, and she had to agree that it was the best she had tasted anywhere.

"They're made with homemade ice cream," he told her.

"He raves about the merchandise because his uncle owns the store," Lot said quietly.

"And *his* brother owns the filling station," Bobby cut in. "When business is slow, he goes around siphoning gas out of cars."

Lot looked embarrassed and blushed slightly. "I wish you'd quit saying that, Bob! People are beginning to believe you." His voice, still undecided on its permanent pitch, cracked and wavered. Bobby and the others laughed, but Lot took it good-naturedly.

"I suppose you've gathered by now that everybody's related to everybody else in this town," Bobby started to explain when a short, rather stocky girl approached the table. She had long, blonde hair that looked a little too dark at the roots to be natural; but that, or any other defect, went unnoticed because of her spectacular build. Beside her, April felt like a stick.

"Hi!" the girl greeted them and pulled out the last empty chair at the table. Before sitting down, she leaned over and rumpled Bobby's hair, as if to identify her private property. Bobby didn't look displeased.

"This is Ellen MacDonald," he said. "April MacKenzie."

"Oh, yes, I think you met my mother the day you arrived," the girl said.

April nodded. She remembered the weasel-faced woman who had seemed to dislike her so much. This girl bore little actual resemblance to her mother, yet there was something in her expression that was similar, something furtive about the eyes.

"And how are your aunts?" Ellen asked. It was an innocuous question, but there was a sudden alertness among the others.

"Why, they're fine," April replied.

Now that the door had been opened, Betty stepped in. "Isn't it scary up there? You know, the Castle's such an odd place and all."

Betty had seemed a bit friendlier than the others, and April attributed her question to idle curiosity. But she had a different feeling about Ellen. Before April could reply, Ellen spoke.

"Well, I wouldn't mind living in a castle, even if it had ghosts . . . or witches, as long as I had plenty of money. You're lucky to have a castle *and* wealth."

Mr. Roberts had mentioned that some people believed her aunts were still rich. But April knew now that this wasn't true.

"I don't know what you mean," she said, trying to be civil.

Ellen was about to say something else when Lot chimed in helpfully, "I'll bet you miss California weather if it's really as warm and sunny as the Chamber of Commerce says it is." His pleasant smile made his thin face almost attractive.

April gave him a grateful look, and as she started to reply, the room fairly burst with sound. The siren in the volunteer fire department two doors away was summoning firemen, and the noise was deafening. Most of the boys in the store grabbed their coats and raced for the door. They were volunteer firemen when they weren't in school.

Bobby gave Ellen a wave, then paused beside April and said, "See you here tomorrow."

April glanced at her watch and was startled to see how late it was, realizing she would have to go back without doing the shopping she had planned.

As the boys left, Betty moved over beside Ellen; and a plain-faced girl, Virginia, sank languidly into the chair beside April. She was quite homely, and her theatrical makeup only emphasized the fact. But no one seemed to notice. They saw each other so often, it was doubtful they saw each other at all.

"I guess I'd better go, too," April said. "I have a long walk ahead."

"You'll be back for Hogmanay?" Virginia asked.

"Oh, she'll be back before that," Ellen interjected, her eyes as resentful as her mother's had been. "That is, if she's around. She could just vanish."

"Don't scare her with all that business!" Betty protested. "It's just quieted down, so why stir it up again?"

"She might as well know what she's up against," Ellen replied, undaunted. "There have been visitors who have never returned from the Castle."

"I don't see how anyone could believe that!" April exclaimed.

"We're just trying to be helpful." Ellen suddenly switched tactics and acted friendly. "Strange things happen up on the hill, and you should know about them so you can take precautions." Now she seemed to be repeating her mother's words.

72

"Thanks for your help, but I still don't know what you're driving at," April said.

Ellen reflected for a moment while Betty jabbed her with an elbow and whispered, "Skip it, Ellen!"

"No, it isn't fair not to come right out and tell her," Ellen said finally and turned back to April.

"Just for your own protection, you should know that we think your aunts aren't—uh—regular people. They're witches! Genuine broom and cauldron witches!"

# CHAPTER

# 7

When day was gane, and night was come,
   About the evening-tide,
This lady spied a bonny youth
   Stand straight up by her side.
               *Old Scottish Ballad*

ELLEN'S BOLT OF LIGHTNING stunned April. So the townspeople meant more than eerie atmosphere when they called the MacKenzie place "Witches' Castle." They meant real witches! But April felt no fear, only anger, as she stared into the green eyes of Ellen MacDonald. She wished Ellen would quit being so "helpful." She felt sure that jealousy was behind all this, yet it was ridiculous for anyone who looked like Ellen to worry about competition from the like of her.

Determined to deny Ellen the satisfaction of seeing any reaction, April said calmly, "That's a pretty wild accusation. Can you prove it?"

"I can't, but my mother can! She's seen Elsbeth MacKenzie put a hex on people. And she knows about other things, too," Ellen hinted with just the right touch of mystery.

Even though her charges were bizarre, she uttered them with conviction, and the other girls evidently accepted them as facts.

"My mother used to work for the MacKenzies, and she saw lots of strange things, first hand," Ellen went on. "Why, some of the things she could tell you would make your hair stand on end." She paused for effect, then said in an awesome tone, "So if you know what's good for you, you'll watch your step."

Before April could think of an adequate reply, Ellen added another bombshell. "Maybe you don't know it, but your father left here for good because Old Man MacKenzie accused him of stealing his money. My mother heard them arguing. But actually, it was the witches who took the money and then convinced Mr. MacKenzie his son had stolen it."

Ellen sat back smugly, awaiting the results of this revelation. April's mind was a bramble of confusion, but she steeled herself against showing it.

"Well, thanks for the advice," she said lightly.

"I'm sure I don't have anything to worry about, though. I stopped being scared of bogymen and witches a long time ago." She turned and left abruptly, hoping she sounded more confident than she felt.

April plodded up the snow-covered street as fast as the borrowed, heavy boots would allow her. She would have to come back tomorrow to buy a new pair. Right now, all she wanted was to get away. Witches indeed! She found herself wanting to defend her aunts—in spite of green thumbs and bubbling cauldrons.

Her thoughts were in such turmoil, she didn't see the large woman erupt from the grocery store until she had collided with her. The impact didn't bother the woman, but April felt as if she had ricocheted off a piece of granite.

"Why, it's April MacKenzie!" cried the woman in a loud voice. "I always thought I was big enough to see!" She laughed uproariously at her joke.

April shook her head to make the sidewalk stop spinning. As her eyes began to focus again, she recognized Mrs. Ramsay, the mayor's wife.

"I'm so sorry," April apologized. "I just wasn't looking where I was going."

Mrs. Ramsay studied her rather carefully. "Do you feel all right, my dear?"

"Oh, I'm fine," April replied.

"Is everything all right on the hill? Nothing bothering you?" she persisted.

"Everything's fine."

Mrs. Ramsay eyed her doubtfully. "The mayor and I were talking about you this morning. We feel that, in a way, your welfare is the administration's welfare. We want to be sure you're being taken care of properly. Every man's his brother's keeper, don't you know."

April managed to escape only after listening at length to Mrs. Ramsay's philosophy of the strong being responsible for the weak. What it all boiled down to, she decided, was an excuse for Mrs. Ramsay to meddle in everyone's business. Not knowing what went on at the MacKenzies' seemed to be one of her great frustrations and led her to suspect the worst.

April had almost reached the road leading up to the Castle when she heard her name being called. She turned and saw Mr. Roberts coming up the street in his sleigh with Old Nell at a trot. He pulled to a stop beside her and started chuckling.

"I was in the store when I saw you try to plow Mrs. Ramsay off the sidewalk. Hooo-heee! Looked like a canoe attacking a battleship." He wiped tears of laughter from his eyes. "Been wondering how you were getting along up there." He pointed in the direction of the Castle. "You headed there now?"

April nodded. "I didn't realize it was so late."

"Well, climb in and I'll give you a lift part of the way. Then you'll be home before the sun sets. You shouldn't wander around up there after dark. It isn't safe."

She was grateful for the ride. The road looked twice as long and lonely as it had on the way down. She snuggled under the heavy lap robe in the sleigh and listened to the merry rhythm of the harness bells. They helped to soothe her troubled feelings. "Fitting in" here was going to be more difficult than she had thought, judging from what had happened today.

Mr. Roberts gave her a swift glance, then began chatting about the forthcoming holiday.

"Hope you'll help us celebrate," he said. "My missus is baking her special Pitcaithly bannocks. Makes them only for Hogmanay, and are they good! Mmmmm!" He smacked his lips in anticipation.

April looked at the round little man, a living testament to his wife's good cooking. With a beard, he would be a perfect Santa Claus. He even had a sleigh, although Old Nell was hardly a Dancer or Prancer. The thought of Mr. Roberts and Old Nell sailing over rooftops made her smile.

"Glad to see you a little more cheerful," he remarked. "When things look gloomy, I always say to myself, 'Rufus,' I say, 'this, too, shall pass.' Then I feel better because I know it's true. One day things look sorrowful and the next, bingo! Everything's rosy."

Mr. Roberts's homespun philosophy was corny, but it was comforting. April felt better—until she thought again about Ellen's comments.

"Some people still seem to think my aunts are rich," she said tentatively. The old man took the bait and began talking, as she had hoped he would.

"Well, as I told you the other day, there wasn't much left of Sam MacKenzie's fortune when he died; and knowing how tight he was with money, some folks think . . . well, they think it's still around. He told the miners he was going to leave a good chunk to their pension fund, which isn't too healthy these days, so when your aunts reported there wasn't any money for the fund or anything else, there was some bitterness about it. Not much mining going on around here now—mines all pretty well worked out. Lots of folks don't work regular and have time to speculate on what happened to the MacKenzie money."

"What do most people think happened to it?"

"Well, there're some fancy tales," Mr. Roberts hedged. "One person gives his ideas and somebody else adds his; and first thing you know, all these maybes seem like facts. You know how it is."

"I guess that accounts for some of the things I've heard about my aunts."

Mr. Roberts cleared his throat and said, "I wouldn't put much stock in what you hear." Apparently he already knew what she had heard, so April assumed that the stories about her aunts must be common knowledge.

"Folks seem to get more superstitious when they stay in a little place like Glen Ayr all their lives," he added. "They need to travel—see what it's like in other places. Now I'm lucky. I get railroad passes, and I've been all the way to Niagara Falls. My missus and I went there on our honeymoon. Been down in Virginia, too. It makes a difference in your outlook when you get about, but some folks here haven't been more than fifty miles from home."

He paused, struck by a thought. "You see Mrs. MacDonald in town today?"

"No, but I saw her daughter, Ellen," she replied.

"Oh, ho! So that's it! Don't pay any mind to what she says. Gets all that nonsense from her mother. Della's still carrying a grudge against Miss Elsbeth because of Jock Cameron. It isn't natural after all these years, but there it is."

"What about *Mr.* MacDonald?" April asked.

80

"Oh, he took off long ago. He and Della didn't get on too well, so he just up and left one day. I don't know why, but that seemed to set Della against the MacKenzies more than ever."

He slapped the reins for emphasis. "A grudge acts like a sore. Feeds poison into your system. So you be careful with Mrs. Mac and that Ellen. Tongues as sharp as hayknives!"

They were halfway up the mountain now, and Mr. Roberts reined Old Nell to a stop. "I'm afraid I'll have to drop you here. The train is coming through in a little while, and I have to get back to the station." He checked his big pocket watch. "Somebody might get off today. Lots of families getting together for the holiday. That's the best part of the Daft Days. You'll be all right now, but don't tarry!" He waved and started back to town.

April began walking up the steep road, mulling over all the bits of information she had gathered that day. Glen Ayr's rumor mills were lively, if nothing else was.

As the sun dropped lower in the sky, long, sinuous shadows crept down the mountain. April shivered even though she was warm from the exertion of the climb. The gloomy woods looked forbidding, and she kept turning her head at every sound or movement. Suddenly a tall, black shadow moved through the trees and emerged beside her.

81

She gasped and was ready to scream when she recognized the figure. She might have known it was that weird Andy!

"Didn't mean to frighten you," he apologized. "I was turning over my traps for the night and spotted you. Thought I'd walk along. It's awfully easy to stray off this road because of the snow. And the terrain's pretty rough—fallen timber and sink holes . . ."

She was already annoyed with him for startling her. Now to imply that she needed his help to stay on the road was too much. "Do you always sneak up on people like this?" she asked irritably.

She wasn't sure because of the scarf, but she thought he smiled. "It's habit," he said. "If you spend a lot of time in the woods and fields, you sort of revert to the ways of nature—an improvement over the ways of man, I might add."

"I can't imagine why," she said, ready to argue with him about anything. He had that effect on her. "Man's come a long way since he lived like an animal."

"How do you figure that?"

"Well, for one thing, look at houses. You'll have to admit that even the worst ones are better than a cave."

"Oh, we've developed a lot of skills all right, but I was thinking of something more basic," he explained. "Like the nice balance in nature. Unless man messes it up, everything's checked in some way so it stays within limits. Some animals eat plants, and others kill for food; that's part of the balance. But they seldom turn on their own kind. And they don't pollute the water or erode the soil or deliberately spoil things for future generations the way man does."

He paused and seemed a little disconcerted by his own outburst. April was amazed that this strange creature who skulked through the woods should have such intense feelings. Until now, he had been only an apparition that never seemed quite real. Yet here he was in the flesh, and full of positive ideas that, for some unexplainable reason, she wanted to dispute. Unfortunately, there was nothing she knew less about than nature.

They walked along in silence as she searched for a rebuttal. Suddenly the boy extended an arm and stopped her.

"Don't move!" he whispered and walked slowly ahead of her toward a furry little animal waddling across the road. It was black with two white stripes down its back and bushy tail.

April clapped a hand to her mouth. She didn't have to be a wildlife expert to know a skunk when she saw one. But that stupid boy didn't even recognize it!

As Andy approached, the skunk turned and raised its tail over its back like a flag. The boy stopped still. Then he began talking very gently to the animal and moving forward again. Slowly the tail lowered; and to her surprise, Andy went right up to the skunk and fed it something from his pocket. He motioned for her to join him.

April stayed where she was. If he wants to show off and gets sprayed for his effort, she thought, it'll be all right with me. He probably thinks skunks smell good. But I'm not about to sample its perfume.

The boy looked back at her. "It's all right," he called softly. "This is an old friend. Just come toward her quietly. Skunks never waste their musk. They have to be threatened before they use it."

He spoke with such assurance she didn't doubt the truth of his words. On the other hand, she had no wish to put them to a test, so she hung back.

"Don't be afraid," he said finally, and she thought she detected a slightly mocking tone. He looked at her, and she recognized the challenge in his eyes. It was as if he were proving to himself she was just another simple-minded girl.

Almost involuntarily she moved forward, and this time she was sure his eyes twinkled. She wished he would unwind that ridiculous scarf! She might as well converse with a mummy.

"This is Chanel," he said as April drew near.

"She stops by our house for a handout most evenings." The skunk ignored her and continued to chew on the food Andy had contributed.

April sniffed. "She doesn't smell skunky."

"No, they never do. She's quite neat and clean." He ran his hand over the long fur, and Chanel seemed to enjoy the attention.

"Her scent comes from glands under her tail. When she means business, she raises her tail, then does a forward flip as she sprays. Her aim's unbelievably accurate. But she won't use her weapon except in self-defense. It's a shame she has such a bad reputation because she really doesn't deserve it. She minds her own business unless someone bothers her first."

April stooped down beside the boy, and a stick cracked loudly under her foot. The skunk's tail flew up; and, instinctively, April froze. As Andy cooed reassurance to the wary animal, her flag lowered to halfmast and she waddled off into the woods.

April breathed a great sigh. "I thought sure I'd be wearing Chanel Number Six, or whatever her brand is."

"Number One; she stands alone," he replied with a laugh. "But it would take more of a threat than a stick cracking to make her react. She's rather level-headed, doesn't fly off too easily."

April realized that he was discussing the skunk

in the terms he would use for a person. Maybe he was so far out he thought animals were people. She turned to study him at close range to see if she could detect a wild gleam in his eye or some other sign of unbalance. He was watching her, so she looked away again, but not before she noted that his eyes weren't black after all. They were deep blue, almost purple. Even this discovery bothered her. It was further evidence that she couldn't come up with any right answers about this boy. He was an enigma.

"You roam these woods all the time?" she asked as they walked on. She had almost said, "haunt these woods," but had caught herself in time.

"I have to run the farm," he replied, "but I spend as much time here as I can manage." He looked around at the white woodland. "This is home to me."

"But don't you get lonesome?" April hated to be by herself and tried to avoid it at all costs.

"It's hard to get lonesome in a busy place like this," he told her. "Stand still for just a minute and look and listen."

She stopped, but failed to see or hear anything except the rustle of bare branches in the wind. "Look over there!" He pointed to a tree where two squirrels in a playful mood were chasing each other around a tree.

86

Then with a slight motion, he indicated a thicket not far from the road. As she stared at it, her eyes gradually picked out the form of a deer standing motionless, observing them. A noisy bluejay shrieked overhead, and the deer flipped its white tail and bounded away.

"See there, in the snow?" Andy showed her small paw prints. "Fox. We're probably being watched right now by at least a dozen pairs of eyes. So you see, you're seldom alone in the woods."

These animals weren't the sort of company she had in mind, but it seemed useless to tell him that, for she felt he wouldn't understand.

They had almost reached the Castle when the boy said, "I have a few more traps to turn. Birds will freeze if they get caught now." With that, he left her. She watched him start through the woods, then vanish—as if he'd never been there. Once again she had the strange feeling that he was a figment of her imagination.

When April opened the heavy door of the Castle and went in, the raven swooped down from its high perch and sat on the back of an ornately carved chair. It was then that April noticed the matching chair was missing. And so was the table that had sat between them. That they had both been there when she left for town, she was almost sure.

"Car-r-runk! Car-r-runk!" the raven croaked,

his shaggy throat feathers moving in and out. He seemed very agitated.

A loud, metallic banging echoed through the great hall, followed by the sound of falling stones. Unless she was hearing things as well as seeing them, someone was trying to knock down the Castle!

# CHAPTER

# 8

Thus ev'ry kind their pleasure find,
  The savage and the tender;
Some social join, and leagues combine;
  Some solitary wander:

*Robert Burns*

WITH THE NOISE to guide her, April made her way to the east wing of the Castle. She had noticed when she first arrived that one of the towers in that wing had lost some of its stones—from neglect, she thought. Now she wondered if the stones could have been knocked down deliberately, just as someone was knocking them this minute.

She opened the entrance to the first tower and

was about to ascend the narrow, stone steps when Aunt Milly appeared, more flustered than usual. She hurried down the steps, and April had to back down before she could see what was going on.

"We were—uh—just doing some work on the stones," Aunt Milly explained as she wiped her hands on her apron. Her wispy hair stuck out all over, and there were smudges of dirt on her face and hands. "I'll wash up and get us a bite of supper."

She steamed along to the kitchen, propelling April before her, and her steady flow of conversation forestalled questions. In the kitchen, Genevieve snored on the hearth, and the saw-whet owl dozed on a curtain rod. April didn't know where Mad was lurking; and, oddly enough, it didn't worry her so much as before. She had other problems now.

Aunt Elsbeth soon appeared; and she, too, was disheveled and dusty. April's curiosity grew more intense by the minute, but neither aunt made further mention of their "work on the stones." She resolved to explore that tower at the first opportunity.

Her aunts poured water into basins and began washing their hands. "Papa always said we had the best water in the county," Aunt Milly said. "Comes from a spring in the cellar, and Papa built right over it. But sometimes I wish he'd piped it upstairs so we didn't have to carry it. Guess I'm getting lazy like Genevieve," she chuckled.

"Did you enjoy your trip to town?" Aunt Elsbeth asked, and they both looked apprehensive as they awaited her reply.

April had considered asking her aunts straight out about what she had heard; but now that she saw the worry in their faces, she thought better of it. They were undoubtedly aware of the stories told about them. This may have been why they didn't want her to go into town in the first place. She decided to put their minds at ease.

"I met a group of young people in Thompson's drugstore. They were all talking about plans for Hogmanay," she said offhandedly and watched relief spread over their features. "This certainly is a big holiday around here. But I can't get used to the idea of having a Yule dinner on New Year's Day."

"That reminds me," Aunt Milly spoke up. "We must make plans for our dinner. It should be extra special this year—to celebrate both the holiday and your arrival."

"Yes, it should be special!" Aunt Elsbeth agreed enthusiastically.

April was touched. It had been so long since anyone wanted to do something "special" for her. Her aunts were peculiar, she had to admit, but they were kind, too.

She mentioned Mrs. Roberts's culinary feats, as related by Mr. Roberts, and Aunt Milly's excitement almost swept her away.

"Pitcaithly bannocks! Why, we haven't made them for ages! However did we forget about them, Elsbeth?"

Aunt Elsbeth shook her head. "We always had them when Mama was alive. We still have that recipe somewhere, Millicent."

"But what are they?" April wanted to know.

Both aunts looked at her in surprise. "You've never had Pitcaithly bannocks?" Aunt Elsbeth asked. "Well, we'll have to remedy that."

Aunt Milly began rummaging in a drawer full of papers, balls of string, bits of yarn, and odds and ends. It looked like utter chaos, but in a few minutes she waved a yellowed sheet in triumph. "Here it is! Mama's recipe!"

"But what are they?" April asked again.

"Why it's shortbread fancied up especially for Hogmanay." She spread her hands. "They're impossible to describe; you have to taste them. And taste them you shall!"

They ate a simple supper of oatmeal topped with real cream, dried fruits that had been cooked in some unusual liquid, and bread and cheese. Her aunts' expertise at the cauldron seemed to carry over to their cooking for meals. But April was careful not to check too closely into their recipes.

If the ingredients were anything like the stuff in their brews, she would never be able to enjoy their food again.

April and Aunt Elsbeth washed the dishes while Aunt Milly sat by the fire and knitted on something that was almost as long as Andy's scarf. April kept yawning and was glad when her aunts lit three kerosene lamps and they all started upstairs.

Before getting into bed, April endured the cold to dig around in her little jewelry box. She pulled out her mother's ring, her last link with the home she once knew. She found it reassuring to hold it and to know it was still there. Then she placed it carefully in a cut glass pin dish on the old-fashioned dresser where she could see it every day.

April wriggled under the covers so they wouldn't come untucked at the sides. Her jaunt into town had left her very tired, but she wasn't ready to sleep. First she wanted to see what was going on in that tower. And as soon as her aunts were asleep, she would. She fought to keep her eyelids from closing, but it was impossible. Sleep won easily.

Suddenly she sat up, still groggy, but awake enough to know that something had startled her. She rubbed her eyes and looked around. Darkness had dissolved and dawn was lacing misty, red ribbons through the sky. April wondered what could have awakened her at this hour. Probably a stupid bird making a racket, she thought. She sank back on the pillow, only to bound up again as pebbles rattled against the windowpane.

She jumped out of bed, grabbed her robe, and went carefully to the window. There on the ground below her stood Andy—stocking cap, scarf, and all. April was annoyed. Didn't he ever go to bed? And how did he know which room was hers? She had never known anyone so meddlesome.

April opened the window and leaned out. "Have you any idea what time it is?" she called in a hoarse whisper.

"I know it's awfully early and I'm sorry to bother you, but I need some help. Will you come down?" The suppressed excitement in his voice betrayed his outward calm.

"What is it?" she whispered.

"I'll tell you when you come down," he whispered back. "Don't want to wake your aunts."

She closed the window and looked at the bed. "If I had any sense, I'd go back to sleep," she told herself. "But Andy does seem stirred up." She began putting on her clothes, telling herself that since she was wide awake now, she might as well see what he wanted.

Andy was waiting when she emerged from a little door just below her room. "This way," he said as he hurried along the path to the barn. "I have something back here that I can't quite handle by myself." He hesitated. "I was afraid if I told you what it was, you wouldn't come."

She looked at him suspiciously. "It's not another skunk?"

He laughed. "No, nothing like that. But I'd rather not tell you—just let you see for yourself."

April wasn't at all sure this was a good idea. Only an animal could arouse his interest this much, and it might be anything from a dragon to a mouse. But she trudged behind him as they passed the old stone barn and climbed over the fence near the bird traps.

"See it!" he cried, his excitement breaking through now. "In the trap!"

April looked, but failed to see anything at all. Then something moved, something white that was hard to see against the snow. As they came closer, she gasped in amazement. Crammed into a trap was a large, white bird. The trap was much too small for its great bulk, so there it sat, unable to move forward or back.

"What in the world is it?" she asked.

"A snowy owl! The first I've ever seen. They seldom come this far south; and when they do, they usually stick to the coast or open ground. They never show up in woods like this. Must have been blown off course by that big storm we had about a week ago."

She came closer and knelt down beside the trap

95

for a better look. The bird had appeared completely white at first, but now she saw pale, dusky bars across its back, head, and rounded tail. The owl turned its large, yellow eyes full upon her and glared savagely. It seemed to be blaming her for its predicament.

"A beauty!" Andy breathed and seemed almost reverent in his admiration of the creature. "Probably a male—must be about twenty-five inches long—not in very good shape."

"How did it ever get squeezed in there like that?"

"Went in after a mouse, most likely. Always plenty of mice around the traps because of the grain. He must have been pretty desperate to risk going into the trap, but if you're hungry enough, you take chances. We'll have to get him out, but I want to band him before we let him go."

"We!" she cried. Her role in this strange mission was finally coming to light. "You certainly don't expect *me* to hold that man-eater while you band it, do you?"

"No," he said calmly. "I was hoping you would band it."

April could hardly believe her ears, but obviously he was serious because he opened his bag of bands and began arranging his equipment.

"Look at the size band this fellow takes—number eight!" He held up an aluminum ring that looked a dozen times larger than the one he had applied to the whitethroat.

She refused to be sidetracked. "What do you mean, you were hoping I would band it? I scarcely know a bird from a plane, much less how to band one. How can you say, 'You band it,' just as if you were saying 'Please pass the potatoes'? You must be out of your mind!"

Andy finished recording the band number in his notebook, then looked at her. Again she recognized the challenge in his eyes: was she or wasn't she a dim-witted female with as much depth as a bird bath? He certainly knew how to play on her ego.

"Holding him will be tricky," he went on, ignoring her objections, "so I'll do that. All you need to do is slip this band around his right leg and squeeze it with these pliers until the two ends meet. Nothing to it."

She thought he smiled encouragement, but couldn't be sure with that dumb scarf wound around his neck like thread on a spool.

"Sounds easy, the way you tell it," she said glumly.

He handed her the band and pliers—and a sweater. "You plan to dress him, too?" she asked.

Andy chuckled, then became serious as he contemplated the task he was so anxious to carry out successfully. "The sweater's to cover his head. It'll

**97**

quiet him and protect you from his beak, although you don't have to worry much about that. The real business end is his feet. Those talons are deadly weapons—so stay clear of them. Okay?"

She gulped and nodded, trying not to panic at the prospect of meeting this wild thing face-to-face, or worse yet, foot-to-face.

"He's stuck in the trap headfirst so, luckily, I'll be working from behind him. After I get him out, you toss the sweater over his head, then the banding should be simple."

She tried to convince herself of its simplicity while he pulled on heavy, leather gloves and set to work. Reaching into the open end of the trap with both hands, he pinned the owl's wings firmly against its body. Then, carefully moving the creature from side to side so its feathers wouldn't get caught in the wire mesh, he slowly withdrew it from the cage. Now that its only restraint was Andy's hands clasped around its body, the owl used the opportunity to swivel its head and grab the end of a glove.

"His beak can't do any damage through these gloves," Andy said.

The bird thrashed the air with its feet, spreading its toes and contracting them into knots as it sought to drive the fearsome talons into its captors.

"Put the sweater over its head—quick!" Andy said a little breathlessly.

He has more than he bargained for this time, April thought. He's got a tiger by the tail, and it's too late to let go. She approached cautiously from behind, yet the owl was staring at her. He seemed able to turn his head completely around, just as the saw-whet had done.

She moved closer, noticing the beak almost hidden in the thick feathers of his face. Then she looked into those fantastic yellow eyes again. They blazed with such hatred, a chill went through her body from head to toe. It was almost a relief to toss the sweater over those accusing eyes.

Immediately the bird became quiet, its feet motionless. While maintaining his firm grip on the powerful wings, Andy tilted him slightly so that his legs were thrust forward.

April picked up the band, but the sight of those feet at close range dissolved all pretense of courage. White feathers covered his legs to the very end of his toes where the black-tipped, vicious-looking talons were barely visible. If her arm came within range, they would pierce the flesh to the bone.

"I—I can't get close to those!" she protested.

"Yes, you can," Andy told her gently, but firmly. "Don't try from the front, but come stand beside me. That's good. Now reach out with your left hand and take a firm hold on his leg."

April licked her lips and took a deep breath.

99

Summoning all of her willpower, she extended her hand and clamped onto the leg. The feather-trousers were soft and fluffy, but she could feel the strong muscles and ropelike sinews beneath them. She tightened her grip.

Andy spoke quietly and with the utmost patience. "Slip the band on its leg. That's it—hold it with the fingertips of your left hand. You're doing fine! Now, use the pliers to squeeze the band. Good girl!"

The deed was done, and April felt sick as nervous reaction set in. How did she ever get mixed up with such a crazy stunt!

"Get behind that tree," Andy ordered. "I'm going to release him, and he could attack you. These fellows can get tough if they think they're menaced, but this one's probably too hungry to bother."

April obeyed willingly as Andy placed the bird on a snowbank. After he flipped the sweater from its head, he lost no time in joining her behind the tree. The owl didn't fly immediately, but sat twisting its head as if to get its bearings. Then it ruffled its feathers a few times, spread its wings almost six feet wide, and soared silently into the sky.

They watched in awe as the great bird circled overhead, beating the air without sound and seemingly without effort. The gray curtain of dawn had now lifted on a red winter sunrise. The color washed over the owl, tinting the white feathers pink and edging them in gold. It was a magnificent sight. April felt she had glimpsed something a little beyond mortal limits.

After the pale form turned eastward and disappeared, she and Andy remained very still, reluctant to break the spell. Until that moment, banding birds had meant little to her, just another strange activity of this strange boy. Now it was different. She had actually touched this bird that consorted with the wind and stars and had given it a band to wear forever.

"Where's he headed?" she whispered finally.

Andy turned back from the sky. "Probably to the coast. In the spring, he may make it back to the Arctic where he belongs—if he gets enough to eat."

"But what does he find to eat in the Arctic? There can't be much there."

"Lemmings mostly. But they get scarce about every four years, and these birds come farther south for food. Then they eat mice—or ducks and other birds if they're really hungry."

They walked in silence toward the Castle. "I hope he makes it back home," she said, and Andy flashed her a look of understanding.

"I'm sorry about waking you up this morning, but you can see how it was." He hesitated. "Want to help band some more birds?"

She didn't answer immediately. Banding the owl had been oddly satisfying—and that's what worried her. Sensible people didn't roam around chasing birds. She could become as odd as the rest of the inhabitants of this mountain without even realizing it. Before long people would be pointing her out as "that nutty MacKenzie girl." No, this life wasn't for her. She wanted to do *sane* things, and be with *normal* people.

"No, I don't think so," she said quietly, answering Andy's question.

"Well, thanks for your help. I'm awfully grateful for what you did."

She knew without looking that he was gone.

Her aunts, busily getting breakfast, looked up in surprise when she walked into the kitchen. They thought she was still in bed. Her news of the owl left them as excited as Andy had been, only noisier. They were still exclaiming over her adventure when she went to her room to freshen up.

As she brushed her hair before the mirror over the big dresser, she made a decision. As soon as the chores were finished, she would go into town. Bobby wanted to see her today, and the prospect of their meeting brightened the morning. When she was with him, she could forget these weird surroundings. And, unlike Andy, he seemed perfectly normal!

She put down the brush and glanced idly toward the pin dish where she had left her ring. It wasn't there! She picked up the dish to be sure, then searched the dresser top carefully. There was an old acorn she hadn't noticed before. But the ring was gone!

# CHAPTER

# 9

"My mither is a queen," he says,
  "Likewise of magic skill;
'Twas she that turned me in a dove,
  To fly where'er I will."
                    *Old Scottish Ballad*

For the second time, April trudged down the rough mountain road toward town. Her first trip had been brightened by her encounter with Bobby. Now no one crossed her path, and the riddle of the missing ring weighed on her sagging spirits.

She remembered something Aunt Milly had said about Gabriel keeping a lookout for intruders. Only she had said "someone," as if she meant one particular person was an intruder. Could that "someone" have been Andy? It would be just like her aunts to protect him even if he were a thief.

As soon as April reached Glen Ayr, she headed for the little shop that claimed to be a department store. There she bought a pair of boots and a rose-colored wool scarf for her head. Prices were low compared with California, but her small supply of cash was sadly reduced just the same. She had been tempted to toss the old boots and cap into the nearest trash can, then thought better of it. Her aunts would promote another twenty years of wear out of them, so she had the clerk put them in a bag, while she wore the new items.

April found Thompson's drugstore unexpectedly quiet. Of the gaggle of young people usually there, only Lot was present, giving rapt attention to a science fiction paperback he had borrowed from a rack.

"Hi!" April said twice before he looked up. "Where's everybody?"

With an effort, Lot tore himself away from another time and planet to reply, "Oh, they're helping decorate trees in the square. Bob got hold of some nice ones, probably conned somebody into donating them. Anyway, that's where the gang is now."

April knew where the trees came from, but said nothing. They were for a good cause.

After several false starts, Lot asked, "Want a soda?"

There was something appealing about this undersized, shy boy that aroused her motherly instincts. She wanted to protect him, only she wasn't sure from what. She accepted his invitation and sat down.

"How come you aren't in the square, too?" she asked.

He stuck out a bandaged hand. "Cut it yesterday helping my mother chop nuts for cakes. A dumb thing to do during the holidays," he said with disgust and sat back quietly studying her, his thick glasses giving him an owlish look. "You coming into town for Hogmanay?" he asked.

"I want to," she said while he nervously flipped the corners of the book.

"You'll like it!" he blurted, but it was obvious he had something else on his mind and hadn't yet worked up the courage to say it.

He riffled the pages again before he said in a sudden rush of words, "I really shouldn't tell you this . . . I don't want to worry you, but there's a lot of talk going around. People are saying—uh—all sorts of things about your aunts."

"Oh, that!" April smiled with relief. "That doesn't bother me. I've heard all that business about witches. I'm getting used to it."

"But this is something new," he said earnestly as he leaned across the table. "People have been telling tales about the Castle for years, but this is different—more serious. I guess it started with the rumor that a peddler had disappeared up there. Everyone said that strange things had always happened on the mountain, but when people started disappearing, it was time to do something about it. The talk died down for a while. Now it's started up worse than ever. Mrs. MacDonald keeps saying that your aunts practice black magic. No one'll admit believing her, but they do just the same."

He sat back, looking apologetic for having told her this.

"But what were my aunts supposed to have done with the peddler? Turned him into a frog?"

Lot shrugged. "Nobody's too clear about that. Mrs. MacDonald says . . ."

"That Mrs. MacDonald has all the charm of a cobra!" April sputtered. "I don't know why anyone would believe a thing she says!"

"She used to work at the Castle so she's considered an authority on what goes on up there. She's been telling everyone for years that your Aunt Elsbeth turns herself into a big, black bird—all sorts of queer things like that. Personally, I think *she's* nutty, but people believe her. I guess it's because the Castle's a spooky place, and your aunts never show up in town or even bother to deny the tales."

"Maybe they don't know about them," April suggested.

"Maybe, but everyone seems to think they do. Andy Fergusson might not tell them, but his grandmother wouldn't hesitate. She has trouble getting around because of her rheumatism or something, but that doesn't stop her from finding out everything that's going on. What a character! She's nosey, but she's usually nosey for a reason. I'll have to give her that. Creates an awful rumpus sometimes. Have you met her yet?"

April shook her head. "No, and I don't know Andy very well," she said slowly, remembering her missing ring.

"Not long ago," Lot continued, "Mrs. Fergusson got wind of a plot some busybodies were hatching up to get your aunts out of the Castle. She was furious! She got Andy to bring her to town in that strange contraption he drives, and she went right to the mayor. Told him what she thought of such a scheme. I doubt if it did any good, though, because the mayor does whatever his wife says, and it was partly Mrs. Ramsay's idea. And, of course, Mrs. MacDonald's. I hear Mrs. Fergusson's been trying to give her a piece of her mind, too, but she can't corner her. I'd like to be there when she finally catches up with her."

108

"But why do they want to get my aunts out of the Castle?" April asked.

"As far as I can make out, Mrs. Ramsay and Mrs. MacDonald, and some others, plan to turn the Castle into the mayor's official residence—and maybe a tourist center. Sort of like the White House."

"That's impossible!" April exclaimed. "My aunts wouldn't give up their home. They've lived there all their lives."

"They may not have any choice. If their taxes go up and they can't pay them, the town can take it over. Anyway, that seems to be the general idea. The tax assessor went up there awhile ago, to look things over, but something happened and he won't go back. That won't stop them though."

"I can't believe it!" April said in a stunned tone. "My aunts wouldn't have any place to go if they lost their home."

"Well, they would, but they probably wouldn't like it. You see, they'd be sent to Clear Spring, to a hospital and home for old folks over there. These do-gooders say that since your aunts are senile, they'll be better off where someone can keep an eye on them. Of course, this peddler thing played right into their hands. Convinced more people that your aunts might be a real menace. They were all set to act when you showed up. That complicated things because they hadn't counted on any relatives being around. But they're taking care of that."

"What do you mean?"

Lot looked uncomfortable. "Well — uh — now they have another excuse. They say your aunts aren't fit guardians for you—an 'impressionable young girl'—I think that's what they called you."

They sat in silence for a few minutes as April tried to comprehend this new turn of events. She had no idea that the web of gossip around her aunts could actually imprison them.

Lot cleared his throat. "You won't mention that I told you this, will you?" he asked anxiously. "I wasn't supposed to hear it, only people always think I'm deaf just because I've got my head in a book."

"I won't tell," April promised. "But why are you? Telling me, I mean."

"I dunno," he said, embarrassed. "It didn't seem right not to. Besides, if you can prepare your aunts for what's going to happen, it won't be so much of a shock."

April looked at him with new appreciation. "Thanks for letting me know," she said.

He smiled shyly. "That's all right . . . anything I can do. I just hope you don't have to go back to California."

"I won't go back without a fight!" she told him

110

with conviction. The words were spoken before she fully realized the step she had taken. For the first time, she had aligned herself with her aunts; their fate was now her fate, even if they turned out to be genuine "broom and cauldron witches," as Ellen had called them. They were her family, and they needed her. What's more, she was growing fond of them.

She turned to Lot and asked him point-blank, "Do you think my aunts are witches?"

The question wasn't fair; she knew that as soon as she had asked it, but Lot took it in stride.

"Dunno," he said honestly. "I've never met the ladies. But they do mind their own business—something most of the people in this town never do."

His intense feeling surprised her. There was more behind that meek exterior than she had suspected.

He cocked an eye at her and asked blandly, "Do you think they're witches?"

The question might have disconcerted her earlier, but not now. "It's a funny thing, but that doesn't seem to matter anymore. They're just two kind people who are victims of a cruel plot, and I'm going to do something about it. Only I'm not sure what."

"Good for you!" said Lot.

111

There was admiration in his expression and something else—something she could sense, rather than see—but it bothered her. She liked this boy, not in a romantic way, but as a friend, or perhaps as the brother she had never had. She wished he would think of her as a sister.

"I'd better go," she said quickly and headed for the town square, only vaguely aware that Lot had joined her. She had come to town primarily to see Bobby, and now she realized that he was the very person who might be able to help the most in this serious situation involving her aunts. Bobby liked her, she could tell; and she trusted him despite his mother's troublemaking. In fact, he might persuade his mother to change her mind about taking over the Castle.

"Have you known Bobby long?" she asked Lot.

"All my life," he replied. "Almost everybody in this town grew up together. It doesn't change much."

"He's very popular," she commented, probing for more information, but Lot remained noncommittal.

"Yeah, Bob's okay," he said. Then added casually, "Ellen likes him, too."

April gave him a sharp glance to be sure he wasn't making fun of her. She should have known better; he was simply trying to warn her about the competition. Lot was very perceptive.

"Hi!" Bobby called out as they approached the square. "You're just in time to miss the hard part, but we could still use another pair of hands," he said, laughing. As usual, Lot's presence went unnoticed.

One look at Bobby and April's knees felt wobbly. No one had ever had such an effect on her before. All at once there seemed less reason for her to worry about anything. Bobby was so self-confident, she could relax. With him on her side, how could she lose?

The group that had sat at their table in the drugstore yesterday was here now, busily trimming the trees. Except for Ellen, they seemed friendlier today. While Lot sat by watching, April joined them in the decorating; and by late afternoon, the square had taken on a festive appearance. Suddenly she realized that the sun was low in the sky. It was hard to think of practical things like time when she was with Bobby.

"It's late. I have to leave," she said, hurriedly gathering up her package.

Ellen was leaning against Bobby, feigning exhaustion from the work. "Don't rush," she said. "If you aren't home by midnight, a big bird will swoop down and carry you back."

Everyone laughed but Lot. Then, surprisingly, Bobby said, "Lay off, Ellen."

Ellen straightened up and flashed him an angry

look. "I'm sure April doesn't mind if I spill a few well-known secrets. There *is* a big, black bird that lives in the Castle, isn't there, dear?" she asked sweetly.

"It's only a raven . . ." April began, but Ellen cut her short.

"And your aunts do make all sorts of brews in a big, black cauldron, don't they?"

Everyone had gathered around now to witness this exchange. April tried to shrug off the questions, but Ellen fired away relentlessly until Bobby intervened.

"Leave her alone, Ellen! She isn't responsible for anything her aunts do!"

April wasn't too happy about the way he phrased this, but she appreciated his help just the same.

Ellen made no attempt to hide her anger. The fact that Bobby had publicly taken sides with this intruder enraged her, and she lashed out. "Okay, Sir Galahad. They're her family, don't forget. If there's nothing odd about her, then there's nothing strange about the Castle. But I notice you haven't rushed all the way up there, not even to 'borrow' trees."

Bobby flushed, but she didn't stop. "Surely you aren't going to let her walk home all alone when a big, brave soul like you could escort her there. What can happen if she's along?"

114

The group watched in fascination, but April wanted to hide. Bobby would hate her for being the cause of such a scene.

He waited irresolutely, only his eyes revealing his anger. Finally he said in a low voice, "I had every intention of taking April home. And I'm sure you'll want to come along, too. That is, if you aren't afraid something will jump out and say, 'Boo!' "

Pleased by the effect this remark had on his audience, he added, "And what's more, I'm going to fetch April for Hogmanay!"

Ellen looked chagrined, aware that she had pushed him too far.

"Come on, everybody!" he called. With laughter and jokes about witches and spells, they piled into the sleigh standing in the square, and Bobby untied his piebald horse. April wished someone had bothered to ask her if she wanted to be driven home. Now it was too late to refuse. Reluctantly she climbed into the sleigh, and Lot got in beside her. She hoped things were quiet on the mountain—that Aunt Elsbeth wasn't stewing up more herbs, or Gabriel didn't decide to attack anyone, or . . . There was no end to the things that could add more fuel to the rumor fires.

"Let's go!" cried Bobby. "Giddap, Jezebel!"

A more observant group had seldom traveled

the narrow mountain road. Most of them had learned at an early age to stay away from the mountain, partly because their parents were superstitious about it and partly because old Mr. MacKenzie used to back up his no-trespassing signs with a shotgun. Not that he had ever shot anyone, but he had scared some of them out of a year's growth.

As they neared the top, the talk died down; and an apprehensive silence descended.

Suddenly the stillness was shattered by a cry from Ellen. "Look up there!"

All heads turned toward the sky where a bird circled directly over them. "It's her! I know it is! One of the witches turns herself into that black bird! My mother says so, and she's seen it with her own eyes!" Ellen was almost hysterical, and her panic infected the others.

"I don't think I want to go any farther," Virginia wailed.

April recognized the wedge-shaped tail and broad wings that ended in feather-fingers. "It's only a raven," she said, annoyed with Ellen. She suspected there was more malice than fear behind her outburst. And it was just as well they didn't know that the bird usually frightened her, too. But she certainly couldn't believe that he was her aunt! That was really ridiculous.

Without warning the raven floated down and

116

landed right on the horse's back. Jezebel started, then reared up on her hind legs, tumbling the sleigh's occupants about like tenpins. Bobby pulled frantically on the reins crying, "Whoa! Whoa!" The horse paid no attention, but whirled about and headed down the mountain at top speed.

April had clung to the sleigh to keep from falling out until she realized that the safest place was on the ground. Before she could gather the courage to jump, someone gave her a mighty shove, and she landed facedown in a snowbank. She sat up in time to see the sleigh careening toward the steep slope, everyone screaming hysterically. All except Lot. She caught a glimpse of him looking back anxiously, and she knew who had pushed her.

April rushed to the crest of the slope, expecting to see bodies strewn over the snow. Instead, the horse had slowed down, but no one seemed to notice. The screaming continued at full volume.

When she turned back, Mad was standing in the road, cocking his shoe-button eyes at her. "It's all your fault!" she said indignantly as she brushed off the snow. "You've really messed up things now! By the time Ellen gets through telling about this, it'll sound like Frankenstein and Bluebeard rolled into one."

To her amazement, the bird fluttered into the air and settled on her shoulder.

"Shoo!" she snapped. It hopped to the ground and strutted off toward a tree by the road where it croaked out its displeasure.

In the pauses between the noisy "car-r-runks," April could hear a soft chuckle.

# CHAPTER
# 10

Proper he was, both young and gay,
   His like was not in Fyvie,
Nor was ane there that could compare
   Wi' this same Andrew Lammie.

*Old Scottish Ballad*

"THIS IS JUST TOO MUCH!" April said. She had trailed the raven to the tree; and there, just as she suspected, was Andy, trying unsuccessfully to stifle his laughter.

"Are you responsible for all this trouble?" she asked angrily.

"I had nothing to do with it, so help me!" Andy replied. "It was pretty funny, though. All those characters, including the great football hero, having a fit over a bird." He began laughing again.

119

"I don't see anything funny in scaring those kids like that," she said in an icy tone. "When that horse bolted, they could have been killed!"

"Oh, they're all right. That mare couldn't run down the mountain if she wanted to—it's too steep. And she has more sense than to break her own neck. In fact, she has more sense than most everyone in that sleigh. I know because I used to own her. Sold her to Mr. MacLeod, and then Bobby got her in some sort of deal. He does a lot of wheeling and dealing."

It was evident that Bobby wasn't one of his favorite people.

"That's all beside the point," April said. "It's just very strange that Mad showed up at this particular time and decided to perch on that horse—unless he had some coaching from the sidelines. He even sat on my shoulder. He's never done that before."

"Well, if you must know, I spotted him flying toward town several times today and whistled him back and kept him with me. It just happened I was checking traps over this way when the sleigh came along, and he sailed out to greet you before I had a chance to stop him."

April looked skeptical, yet she didn't believe that he was lying to her.

"By the way," he added, "Raven Mad seems to

120

have taken a fancy to you, so you'd better be sure he doesn't follow you again. If he goes off this mountain, someone's bound to take a shot at him. Most people in town have—uh—strange ideas about him." He gave her a sidelong glance. "I guess you know about that."

She nodded, feeling slightly guilty because some of those very people had accompanied her here.

Andy scraped the snow with the toe of his boot and asked awkwardly, "Do you believe them? You know, about witches and such stuff?"

They had started up the road and walked in silence for a minute or two before she spoke. "Did you know Aunt Elsbeth has a green thumb? I don't mean she has a way with plants—she does of course—I mean an honest-to-goodness green thumb."

Andy looked amused as she sidestepped his question. "Why didn't you ask her about it?" he replied in the blunt manner she found so annoying.

"I was going to, but she seemed a little sensitive about it, especially after Aunt Milly teased her. But green thumbs and normal people simply don't go together, at least not where I come from."

"Most things have a logical explanation. For instance, Miss Elsbeth was using some sort of herb as a dye and got it on her thumb. It'll wear off eventually. But 'normal' people, as you call them,

121

prefer their own cockeyed theories—particularly that bunch of scared rabbits that was just up here."

"They happen to be my friends!" she said with rising indignation. "And they've been nice to me, some of them, anyway. I don't know why you keep picking on them. They haven't done anything to you."

"Haven't they?" She was surprised at the bitterness in his voice. "You don't know what it means to be 'different' in an isolated little place like this. But I don't mind so much being considered an oddball. It's all this superstition that really bugs me. Anything people can't understand is bad, that's their philosophy."

"But they're not all like that," she protested. "Bobby Ramsay isn't. He's very open-minded. He doesn't mind coming up here at all. In fact, he's going to take me into town for Hogmanay." She hadn't meant to tell him this, but he had goaded her into it.

Andy gave her an odd look. "I wouldn't put too much faith in Bobby Ramsay; you may regret it," he said evenly.

When she didn't reply, he went on. "I guess you've heard what his mother and some of the other town meddlers are planning to do about the Castle. Maybe he thinks it will help things along if he becomes friends with you."

122

Her pride was stung now, and she turned on him. "Did it ever occur to you that he might *like* my company? It isn't impossible, you know. Besides, how would you know what Bobby Ramsay or anyone else thinks? You've spent so much time with your stupid animals, you don't know anything about human beings!"

Tears of anger rolled down her cheeks, but she was determined he wouldn't see her cry. Holding her head high, she stalked off, leaving him standing openmouthed on the road.

Before she was out of sight, he recovered enough to call, "Be careful! Stay on the road."

His advice made her all the more angry. Didn't he think she had enough sense to walk up a road? Well, she'd had it with Nature Boy. From now on, he could band his old owls without any help from her!

The sun had dropped behind the mountain, leaving only a golden glow to light her way. April hurried on, forgetting her anger for the moment as she concentrated on reaching home before it became completely dark. She wasn't at ease on this road in the daytime, much less at night.

In front of her now was a high bank of snow, and the road seemed to curve to the left. She hesitated. Somehow this didn't look familiar. She was sure the road went straight up here. But it couldn't, or she would have had to plow through that snowbank on her way down. It must be the half-light that made everything look so different.

She turned to the left and found that the snow wasn't packed very hard, probably because loose snow was constantly blowing off the tree branches. And the road was hard to follow. It seemed to turn again and there, to her amazement, was the setting sun. In the distance, a house snuggled against the hillside, smoke curling from its chimney; and its windows, painted in sunset, shone like squares of gold. She knew she had never been here before. This was the other side of the mountain! While she was in town, snow must have drifted across the road. Instead of bearing left, she should have gone straight ahead after all.

April had partly retraced her steps when something under her foot shifted. As in the slow motion of a dream, she felt herself sinking right down into the ground. It was such an incredible sensation, her mind refused to believe it. Then, instinctively, she screamed and grasped at anything within reach. As the earth swallowed her, she touched an ice-covered object and clung to it. For a few brief seconds, she hung suspended over the dark emptiness beneath her. Her fingers ached, and her arms strained at the sockets. But the heat of her hands made the ice slick. She was slipping!

124

Slowly her hands slid from the edge of the hole and she dropped. With a thud and a loud cracking sound, her feet hit something that checked her fall. It seemed to be a wooden frame of some kind against the side of the hole, but it was so rickety, the slightest movement made it wobble. She stood pressed against the earthen wall and wondered if falling by degrees was any better than going all the way down in one trip.

There was nothing she could do but cry for help. And that was probably hopeless. Who'd hear her? She took a deep breath and screamed, "Help!"

She cried again, and this time the wooden structure responded with a moan. She froze in terror and waited for the worst. The wood held and she relaxed slightly. It would be a long night, if she survived it.

If only she'd been more reasonable with Andy! she thought. He hadn't really insulted her. He had just expressed his opinion of Bobby, so why should she get mad? She couldn't expect the world to bow before the people she liked. What a numb-skull she was!

She risked another cry for help, and the board beneath her swayed ominously. She would have to stand absolutely still or down she'd go. April leaned against the side of the hole and tried not to think about how many hours there were until morning. She sobbed and felt a tremble under-foot.

"Keep your head," she told herself. "If you panic now, you've had it!"

By looking up into the twilight, she could see how far below the surface she was. Maybe five feet, she guessed. But she could see no way out of this terrible, black hole.

Once she thought she heard her name—probably the first sign that she was cracking up. Then it came again. Andy was calling her! She was sure of it!

"Here!" she cried, sending her perch into spasms. She steadied herself with outstretched arms against the dirt wall and waited, fearful that he might not see the hole and fall in, too.

"April?" The word was whispered just above her. It was the sweetest sound she had ever heard. She looked up and saw the silhouette of a head and shoulders thrust out over the hole.

"I'm here," she answered in a tearful voice.

"Take it easy and I'll have you out in no time." Andy sounded so confident, she was certain he would think of something.

"Can you reach this?" he asked.

Carefully she extended one arm, but could feel nothing. Then wool fringe brushed her fingertips, and she clutched a handful. It was Andy's long scarf.

126

"If you can hang on, I think I can pull you up."

She grabbed the scarf with one hand and was attempting to get a grip with the other when she heard a loud rip. The wool strands were tearing. Cautiously she transferred her weight back to the unsteady footing, a wad of fringe still clinging to her hand.

"It's no use," she whispered. "It won't hold me."

"That's all right," he said calmly. "Just thought we'd try that way first because it was quickest. I'm going for some rope now, and I'll be back before you know it. Are you all right?"

"April!" he called in alarm when she didn't answer. "You still there?"

"I'm here," she said with effort. "Hurry!"

She looked up and he was gone. Terror and loneliness took over again. Just having him buzz around up there had made her feel better, but she might as well face the fact that her situation was hopeless. Only a miracle could get her out of here before the rotten wood gave way.

She lost track of time as she waited; it seemed years. And all sorts of crazy thoughts romped through her mind. She had heard this happened to drowning people sometimes. Now it was happening to her—a sure sign that she was doomed.

Gradually she became aware of a dull thud that vibrated the ground, as if an elephant were stamp-

127

ing through the woods. It wouldn't surprise her a bit if Andy actually owned an elephant. But even that wouldn't help her in this predicament.

She waited, but no one appeared at the opening above her. Her mind became even more active. Maybe Andy wasn't coming back because he knew it was hopeless. Or maybe he had to go for miles to find a rope, or . . .

Suddenly he was leaning over the hole again and calling her name. She was so overcome with relief, she couldn't answer.

He had a flashlight this time and saw that she was still there.

"I'm going to lower a rope," he told her. "It has a loop on it, so try to slip it over your head and around your waist."

Andy snaked the rope down toward her and steadied it just over her head. With rescue this close, it would be terrible to fall now. Very deliberately, she raised one arm through the loop, then the other, and let it slide down to her waist.

Andy, watching from his precarious position beside the hole, fed the rope to her as she needed it. "Now hold on with both hands," he directed. "Then it won't get too tight around your waist. Use your feet to keep clear of the side. Ready?"

"You won't let go, will you?" she asked anxiously.

128

"Don't you worry about that! We've got lots of power up here."

She had no idea what he meant and didn't really care so long as he got her out of the hole.

"Here we go!" he told her, and she heard a loud slap. Then, "Easy now! Gee! Haw!"

While all this shouting was going on, April felt the rope tighten around her. She grabbed it with both hands and hung on. It pulled her from her perch and dragged her upward, bouncing her against the wall of her trap. She tried to push away with her feet as Andy had instructed, but it was hard to do, especially when the rope around her middle was so tight she could scarcely breathe. The only thing that kept her from being sawed in half was the heavy jacket her aunts had insisted she wear.

At last her head was above ground. Andy grabbed her under the arms and hauled her clear of the opening, crying, "Whoa! Whoa!" to her unseen benefactor.

He held up the flashlight and looked at her. "Where are you hurt?" he asked with concern.

April loosened the rope and released a great, nervous sob. "Except for being cut in half, I think I'm all right," she said in a wavering voice. "I don't think anything's broken." Without warning, tears began flowing and wouldn't stop.

"It's all over now," Andy kept saying sympathetically. As her sobs tapered off, he admitted, "I was awfully scared myself. Wasn't sure you could hold on while I went home for the rope—and Clyde." He gestured toward a mountain of flesh she could see dimly in the twilight.

He did have an elephant! she thought. With a long, flowing tail and long hair on its legs. "What *is* that?" she asked.

"Our work horse. Genuine Clydesdale from Scotland," he said with pride. "Usually he doesn't move very fast, but tonight I made him practically jet over here. Then he pulled you out."

"Well, I'm terribly grateful to Clyde," she said and meant it sincerely. "And to you, too. I'm sorry I got so mad . . ."

"Let's forget all that," Andy interrupted. "The important thing is that you're safe. Promise me you won't travel this road again except in broad daylight."

"I promise," she said meekly.

"Come on, I'll take you home." He gave her a boost, and she found herself roughly a mile above the ground with her legs sticking straight out as she attempted to sit astride Clyde's barrel-like middle. He wore no saddle, so she grabbed a handful of his thick mane and hung on.

Andy led the horse, not toward the road she had been traveling, but in the opposite direction.

# CHAPTER

# 11

The moon was sinking in the west,
  Wi' visage pale and wan,
As my bonie, westlin weaver lad
  Convoy'd me thro' the glen.

*Robert Burns*

"KEEP YOUR HEAD DOWN," Andy called as he led Clyde from the black woods.

She put her head against the great beast's neck and clung to his mane to keep from bouncing off when he lifted his enormous feet and plopped them solidly down again.

They had entered a clearing, and the white moonlight revealed a well-trodden path that showed up darker than the surrounding snow. It ran down the slope and up the other side to the cottage she had seen just before her fall.

"I live right over there," Andy said, and she realized they were heading toward his house. "Thought you might want to clean off some of the mud before your aunts see you."

April was glad he had reminded her. In all the excitement of her rescue, she had forgotten that she was a mass of mud and scratches, an alarming sight to spring on anyone. "You sure it's all right?" she asked hesitantly.

"Granny's been dying to meet you! She'd have been up to the Castle before this, but she hasn't been very well lately. Rheumatism, you know. But staying home's harder on her than the rheumatism. She misses keeping up with everything—acts like a caged lion."

They traveled down the slope, and April found it even harder to hang on to Clyde. She kept sliding up on his neck.

"That must have been an old mine shaft you fell into," Andy was saying. "These mountains are full of them, but most have been sealed up. Last time I was in that section of the woods, I didn't notice an open shaft. I haven't been there for a while, though, not since last fall at least. It seems to me there used to be a big boulder there someplace. It may have covered that opening and rain or snow dislodged it. Turned that shaft into a real booby trap."

"And I'm the booby that got caught!" April said, disgusted with herself for letting her temper get her into so much trouble.

Andy laughed. "Don't be too hard on yourself. You're learning fast."

"I'd better! Unless I have nine lives, I can't afford any more mistakes like tonight."

"I'll have to see about covering that hole," Andy said. "Animals could fall in there left and right."

"What about people? You could lose half the population of Glen Ayr that way."

"Not a chance! Some of them do a little poaching on the mountain or cut trees, but they do that farther down the slope. No one comes up this far." He hesitated. "Almost no one," he mumbled more to himself than to her.

They had arrived at his home, and Andy helped her dismount. With a slap on Clyde's vast rump, he sent him trotting toward the stables nearby.

"I'll tend to him later," he said and led her to the small house. It now looked quite different from the house in the sunset. Moonlight had turned it ghostly white, but lamplight filled its windows with an orange glow that was warm and inviting. April shivered; she was chilled to the bone.

When Andy opened the door, a little woman struggled out of her chair and came to greet them.

Her salt-and-pepper hair was plaited into a thick braid wrapped around her head; and her bright, blue eyes were so alert, they seemed to send off sparks like the fire. She walked slightly bent, favoring one leg that was stiffened, so that her whole torso tilted at an odd angle.

"Come in, come in!" the woman cried. After a closer look at April, she exclaimed, "Good gracious! You must have been in a fight with a wildcat!"

Andy introduced them. "This is April MacKenzie and this is my grandmother, Mrs. Fergusson, or just plain Granny." He told the woman, "April's had a little accident, and I thought she could clean up a bit before going home. Her aunts would be upset if they saw her like this."

"I daresay!" Granny replied and immediately took charge of the situation. Without any questions about the "accident," she said, "Andy, take her coat and boots outside and brush them off. And you come with me to the kitchen, young lady. You must be frozen!"

"Outside?" Andy repeated.

"Outside!" Granny said firmly. "Can't have that mud in here."

Andy took April's heavy boots and jacket and left.

"That'll keep him out of the way for a while," Granny chuckled. "He's a fine boy, Andy is, if I

134

do say so myself. I have to be firm with him sometimes, but it's for his own good. Of course some
think he's strange because he likes animals better
than people. Takes after his granddaddy there.
But I can't say I blame either. People aren't always
the noblest of God's creatures, not by a long shot!"

As she talked, the woman poured warm water
into a basin and gave April a soft cloth to bathe
her face and hands. The water felt good on her
bumps and bruises, but it made the cuts sting.

"You let your Aunt Elsbeth put some of her
medicine on those cuts when you get home," she
advised. "It smells like the skunk works on Saturday night, but it does the job. Doctors pooh-pooh
it, but what do they know? Now then, here's
a nice, hot cup of tea and some cookies."

She motioned to a chair by the big stove in the
kitchen, and April put her hands and feet as close
as she dared to the iron monster.

"How're your aunts getting along?" Mrs. Fergusson asked as she poured herself some tea. "I try
to keep an eye on them, but I've been laid up
a spell. They won't visit here because they have
some fool notion that folks in town will include
me in their tall tales about the Castle. Humph!"
She made a loud, contemptuous sound. "Wouldn't
bother me one jot or tittle. Now then, how're your
aunts?"

"They're fine," April said uncertainly.

Mrs. Fergusson's keen eyes were on her and seemed to lay bare all her thoughts. "I'm afraid things will get worse up there before they get better," she said finally. "And I hope you can help, because I haven't been much use to anyone lately. Your aunts need someone with both feet on the ground to look after their interests. They belong to a rare breed that finds it hard to think ill of anyone. And that won't get you far today. No, sir!"

She stopped for a swallow of tea. "Somebody's always ready and willing to take advantage," she went on. "Especially some of these folks who think they know what's best for everyone—even the whole world. Why, I wouldn't trust them any farther'n I can kick an anvil!"

There was a pause, and April tried to think of a suitable reply.

But Granny had another question: "Guess you've heard some of the talk about your aunts?"

April nodded, then said, "Some of it seems confusing. I can't understand why Mrs. MacDonald doesn't bury the hatchet after all these years. That Mr. Cameron she was so crazy about didn't marry her, but he didn't marry Aunt Elsbeth either, so why is she making a career out of heckling the MacKenzies?"

A loud "Ha!" seemed to explode from Granny. "That business about Della MacDonald and Jock

Cameron's all hogwash! Della didn't care a fig about Jock, and he hardly knew she existed. No, that's something she cooked up to throw everyone off the trail. She was angling for a bigger catch—and she almost hauled him in. But not Jock. No, sir! You see, he was my youngest brother, so I know what I'm talking about. Now, enough gossip! Get yourself home, or your aunts will be worried to death."

April was completely baffled. "But if it wasn't Mr. Cameron, why is she angry with my aunts? Who was she after?"

"Why, your grandfather, of course! He was old and not quite clear in his head all the time, so Della made the most of the situation. If Elsbeth and Millicent hadn't caught on in time, there would have been a new mistress at the Castle. Ah, here's Andy. Give April her things and get her home in a hurry. Didn't realize it was so late."

April said good-bye, still in a daze over this latest bit of information. Andy helped her into a box-like sled on runners that was hitched to Clyde, and she was thankful she didn't have to mount the horse again. Her bruises hurt more than she cared to admit.

"Thanks for cleaning my boots and coat," she told Andy. "Hope you didn't freeze doing it."

"No trouble. I took care of the stock while I

137

was outside, too. Granny wanted me to make myself scarce. She isn't very subtle, as you probably found out."

"I think she's nice," April said. "She doesn't beat about the bush."

"That's for sure!"

Andy began talking about life with Granny; and almost before April knew it, they had arrived at the Castle. And she hadn't had a chance to quiz him about this strange business of Mrs. Mac-Donald and her grandfather. But right now she would have to face her aunts, and she wished she didn't have to tell them about her fall. They would never want her to go to town again.

When she entered the great hall, a kerosene lamp glowed on the table, but her aunts weren't there. April assumed they had gone to bed, but then she heard the familiar sound of hammers on stone. Only this time, it seemed nearby.

As she crossed the hall, a giant-size rat with a fuzzy tail ran from under a chair and disappeared at the entrance to the east wing. April had to use all her willpower to keep from screaming. Ravens and roosters were bad enough, but she drew the line at rats!

The banging continued, and she traced it to a room behind the hall. She opened the door quietly and saw her aunts, in dustcaps and aprons, prying

138

stones from a corner of the massive wall. Before they saw her, she closed the door again. They were so absorbed in their task, she doubted that they had even missed her. What could they be up to? Obviously they didn't want her to know, or they wouldn't be so secretive about it.

She went to the big door and slammed it hard. Her aunts came bustling into the great hall, wiping their faces on their aprons.

"Well, my dear, I hope you had a fine time in town," Aunt Elsbeth said breathlessly, and both aunts became so involved in explaining their dusty appearance, no mention was made of April's late return. Nor did they notice her scratches in the dim light.

To be on the safe side, April changed the subject. "Did you know there are rats in the Castle? One ran across the hall just now."

"Well! I'll certainly tell Genevieve about that!" Aunt Milly said indignantly. "She doesn't allow rats in here—except Raffles, of course. But then, he isn't a regular rat."

April decided she had had enough for one day and would just as soon not know about any pet rats. She said good-night quickly, and the three of them went to bed.

# CHAPTER

# 12

So may the Auld year gang out moanin
  To see the New come laden, groanin,
Wi' double plenty o'er the loanin,
  To thee and thine:

*Robert Burns*

YELLOW RIBBONS OF SUNLIGHT crisscrossed her bed when April awoke. She glanced at the clock on the fireplace mantel. Eleven o'clock! That was the latest she had slept since her arrival. When she began squirming out of the depths of the featherbed, she discovered she was stiff and sore all over. Her body felt like one big bruise.

She sat on the side of the bed, checking her scraped shins, and shuddered again at the thought of that hole. What a close call she had had! Well, it was over; no use dwelling on it, she thought. She had other problems now—big ones! Mainly, how to keep her aunts from having to give up their own home. Then a happier thought occurred to her. The Daft Days that aroused so much excitement were finally here!

She dressed quickly, trying to ignore her soreness, and hurried downstairs. Both aunts were in the kitchen, buzzing about the old iron stove. They had fed it chunks of wood until the temperature in the big kitchen soared and the ice on the outside of the windows slid off in sheets.

April grew tired just watching them. They moved with the speed of teen-agers this morning, while she felt like a hundred and two.

"We're making some special treats for Hogmanay," Aunt Milly bubbled, then stood still and stared at her niece. "My stars, child! What happened to you? I hope Genevieve or Gabriel didn't do that." She gently touched April's scratched face.

"No, I fell," April replied without adding any details. There seemed little point in worrying her aunts now about last night.

"Oh!" Aunt Milly looked relieved. "Elsbeth will put some of her ointment on those cuts, and they'll heal in no time." She went back to her baking, pulling a hot pan of delicately browned pastries from the oven and sliding in a pan of unbaked ones.

141

"These are my favorites," she said, pointing to some large, fat cookies cooling on the table.

The room was filled with the most tantalizing odors—cinnamon, lemon, ginger, and the pungent sourness of rising yeast bread. April licked her lips and quite forgot her soreness.

"May I help?" she asked.

Aunt Elsbeth answered by tying a big, white apron around her waist. Soon she was elbow-deep in dough and feeling more at peace with the world than she could remember. The warm kitchen was no longer the fearful place it had been on her arrival. Now it was cozy and friendly, with Genevieve sleeping peacefully on the hearth and the saw-whet owl on its favorite curtain rod. Mad had been banned because he couldn't resist walking on the cakes and stealing raisins. And she had seen no further sign of the strange-looking rat she had met last night. She hoped he accounted for Genevieve's satisfied expression.

"Oh, it's going to be a grand holiday!" Aunt Milly predicted as she added more goodies to the pile heaped on the table. She was usually the livelier of the two, but today dignified and reserved Aunt Elsbeth beamed with as much excitement as her sister.

"It's been a long time since we paid attention to such goings-on," she said. "But it's good to smell the cakes baking again. It really takes me back. Remember, Millicent, when Mama was alive, how the great hall would be filled to overflowing with first-footers? Singing and laughing and passing around the wassail? And how we'd go into town and visit all the houses? The sun would be high before we went to bed."

"Aye," replied Aunt Milly, a dreamy look stealing over her face. "Those were bonny times, for sure. And remember . . ."

They were off again with memories of better days and better times. April was glad they had a blanket of pleasant memories to protect them from the cold winds of reality, but the reminiscences only raised more questions in her mind.

The day sped by as she swept and cleaned and waded through the snow to gather greens for decorating. She and her aunts arranged cut branches of pine and hemlock on the mantel in the great hall and stacked oak logs on the hearth in preparation for a roaring fire.

Then they tied sprigs of white-berried mistletoe with red ribbons, and April climbed a rickety ladder to hang them from the huge chandelier in the center of the hall. This wheel-shaped fixture had black, iron candleholders attached to the outer rim as well as to the "spokes." It held forty candles in all, an extravagance her aunts could rarely afford.

143

But tonight the chandelier would be lit! April began to look forward to the lighting with as much anticipation as her aunts.

She still hadn't told them that Bobby had invited her to the festivities in town. So many things had happened last night, she had forgotten to mention it, and now she was afraid they would be disappointed if she left. She had had no idea they would be making such elaborate preparations for their own celebration. But maybe everything would work out. Bobby had said he would call for her at ten because nothing got underway in town until midnight—an odd hour for parties to start, but this was supposed to be a "daft" holiday. Her aunts would be in bed long before ten, so there should be no problem about leaving.

After a simple supper and a nap, April put on her best, and only, wool dress—a bright blue that she thought did something for her eyes. When she finished at the dresser, she glanced once again into the little pin dish to see if, by some miracle, the ring had come back. It hadn't. That was another mystery she would have to figure out, but not tonight. This was a time for fun.

When she came downstairs, Aunt Milly and Aunt Elsbeth were already in the hall, impatient as children on Christmas Eve.

"It's time to light up!" they sang out and moved the unsteady ladder into place.

Both ladies were wearing dresses April hadn't seen before; apparently their best garments, only it had been a long time since they were new. Aunt Elsbeth wore an ankle-length navy blue crepe, and Aunt Milly had on garnet silk, the same length, but with a frilly collar of yellowed lace. Where the ends of the collar met, she wore an unusual brooch—a delicate cameo set in a frame of twisted silver strands.

"Your pin is lovely!" April told her.

Aunt Milly smiled and touched it gently. "It is lovely. It's a copy of Mama's. She inherited hers from her grandmother. It was made special for her in Edinburgh. Mama had a copy made for me, and Elsbeth was to have the original, but . . ."

Her voice trailed off, and she glanced helplessly at her sister, who came to her aid by changing the subject. April wondered what had happened to the other brooch because Aunt Elsbeth wasn't wearing it.

"Use this taper to light the candles," Aunt Elsbeth directed. "We'll hold the ladder." She handed April a long, waxy stick that she had lit in the fire.

With an aunt on either side to brace the ladder, April ascended and touched the flame to each chunky candle. Slowly the swaying fixture began to glow; and when every candle was burning, it was as brilliant as a crystal chandelier.

145

Her aunts looked on in awe, too overcome to speak. Finally Aunt Elsbeth whispered, "I declare! I'd forgotten how beautiful it is!"

While they watched the candleglow, the red and orange flames from the seasoned oak logs leaped high in the fireplace, and the drab room suddenly took on new color and depth of shadow.

"It *is* beautiful!" April said softly. "Sort of like an old oil painting."

This was the way the room must have looked when her grandfather lived here. This was the way it was intended to look. No wonder he was so proud of it, only . . . She glanced around again and had the uneasy feeling that something was not quite right. Her aunts kept switching the furniture around, but even so, some of it seemed to be missing.

Aunt Milly put a fresh, white cloth on a table at the end of the hall, and April helped her arrange plates of the delicious cakes. On the hearth, red apples hissed and sizzled, and a kettle of Aunt Elsbeth's punch simmered over the fire. After a sip, April still couldn't guess what was in it, but it was good! Hot and tangy and fragrant.

She wondered who was going to eat all this food. Her aunts hadn't been very specific about guests, and she had been reluctant to press the point in case it was just wishful thinking on their part. She hoped they wouldn't be too disappointed if no one

146

showed up—except Bobby, of course. That he would come, she was sure. After all, that business with Mad wasn't her fault.

As April and her aunts sat before the blazing fire enjoying the food and drink, she began to feel sorry for people who lived in ordinary houses. Life in a castle had its moments. In her mellow mood, she gave a raisin cake to Mad, who was perched on the mantel. He flew with it to a high rafter where he pecked out the raisins and gave a loud croak of pleasure after each gulp.

It took several nudges from Aunt Elsbeth before Aunt Milly left the room and returned with a tissue-wrapped package.

"A little something for you, April. Happy New Year!"

"Happy New Year! my dear," Aunt Elsbeth added. "And may you be blessed with many more to come!"

April removed the paper and found a long, long scarf—a twin to the one Andy always wore, or had worn. He had ruined his trying to pull her out of that hole.

"Thank you so much," she said earnestly, aware of all the work that had gone into it. Her aunts were so kind, she wished more than ever that she could do something about the problems facing them.

The three of them settled down to a game of

whist, but April's attention was on the clock. It was after ten and Bobby hadn't come. What's more, her aunts showed no sign of sleepiness. They were working up real excitement over the game.

When the big grandfather clock boomed eleven, April resigned herself to missing the parties in town. Bobby's horse must have gone lame, or Ellen had persuaded him not to come, or... Whatever the reason, she was disappointed. Her interest in the game flagged, and the heat dulled her senses. It was an effort to stay awake.

Suddenly she jerked up straight in her chair, and a sharp pain stabbed her neck. She had dropped off to sleep with her head twisted to one side. A gust of cold air swept through the hall, sending a flurry of sparks up the chimney. April rubbed her neck and looked around. Her aunts were no longer sitting by the fire—and the front door was wide open!

She dashed to the kitchen where a lit kerosene lamp, turned very low, provided a faint light. The kitchen door was open, too! She couldn't imagine why the doors would be open in the dead of winter. And where were her aunts? She was about to leave when, from the corner of her eye, she saw the figure of a woman emerge from the shadows and slip through the open door. It wasn't either aunt, she was certain of that. Who could it be? There was something about it that reminded her of Mrs. Mac-

148

Donald, but that was crazy. She wouldn't be wandering around up here. She thought the place was haunted.

April went to the door and peered out. No one was there. She slammed the door shut. What could have happened to her aunts? It didn't seem likely that they'd gone outside, but... She'd see if their coats were in the closet.

The clock was booming twelve as she dashed blindly into the hall—and bumped into someone standing there. A man! Tall and dark.

# CHAPTER
# 13

O Marie, put on your robes o' black,
　　Or else your robes o' brown,
For ye maun gang wi' me the night,
　　To see fair Edinbro town.

*Old Scottish Ballad*

APRIL JUMPED BACK and let out a yelp of fright.

"What kind of New Year's greeting is that?" asked the stranger.

She looked at him closely. There was something familiar about his eyes. And he wasn't a man; he was a boy.

"Andy?" she ventured uncertainly.

"The same," he replied just as Aunt Milly and Aunt Elsbeth burst in.

"Happy New Year!" they cried.

"A first-footer with hair as black as yours, Andy,

is bound to bring us good luck all year!" Aunt Milly exclaimed.

"Just to make sure, I've brought these." He handed Aunt Elsbeth a piece of coal and Aunt Milly, a loaf of bread. "Here's warmth for your house and food for your stomachs. And here's good luck for the entire year," he said as he presented a small cake with green icing to April.

"Oh, my! Thank you!" both aunts said at once.

"Thank you," April mumbled, still shaken by his sudden appearance. "But why are the doors open?"

"To let good luck come in the front and bad luck go out the back," Aunt Elsbeth explained. "And, as you can see, good luck did come in."

"Happy New Year, one and all!" cried a voice she had heard before, and Mrs. Fergusson limped into the hall. "Wanted to be sure Andy crossed the threshhold first," she explained. "If an old hag like me came in first, no telling what would happen. You'd probably have the worst luck on record."

They all laughed and greeted her warmly. "Now Andy here, doesn't really believe in all this," she said, "but he's smart enough not to tempt fate, although he pretends he's doing it to humor me. Of course we could tell him what would happen if he tried experimenting." She turned to the aunts.

"Do you remember the time that Angus Mac-Clure's smart-aleck cousin was visiting here during the holidays? She deliberately became their first-footer—a terrible thing for a girl to do!"

"Aye, it was terrible!" Aunt Elsbeth agreed.

"They sent her packing afterwards!" exclaimed Aunt Milly.

"What happened?" April and Andy asked at the same time, each as curious as the other.

"Why, it wasn't more'n two weeks later that their house burned down," said Granny. "And then the dog died, and Mr. MacClure walked on a nail—had a bad infection. Simply no end to their troubles, just as everybody had predicted."

The three women seated themselves before the fire.

"And do you remember the Stuarts?" Aunt Milly asked. "He was first cousin to Alice McFee in Perth. Now they had quite a time."

April and Andy exchanged glances. A full discussion of the bad luck suffered by Glen Ayr citizens and their near and distant relatives could take all night. She and Andy began serving the cakes and drink. Then as they ate, she studied him in the firelight. This was the first time she had seen his entire face. With his cap pulled down over his ears and his scarf wound around his neck and chin, there was seldom much of his face visible. In a way, he looked as she had thought he would—thin

152

face, strong chin. Only his hair was jet black. She hadn't expected that, not with his blue eyes. She couldn't call him handsome, yet he wasn't unattractive. His features seemed to reflect the rugged independence of his character.

April felt embarrassed about being home after she had boasted that Bobby would brave the mountain to take her into town. But Andy showed no surprise at seeing her still there.

While the ladies were busy reminiscing, he asked tactfully, "Did you change your mind about going into Glen Ayr?"

She nodded, but didn't explain. They sat quietly sampling the cakes, and after a moment Andy said quite casually, "Thought I might go down and join in the fun. Will you change your mind again and come along?"

She was amazed. He never went into town unless it was really necessary; he said so himself. But she was delighted that he wanted to go. Ever since she had arrived in this out-of-the-way place, she had been hearing about the celebration of Hogmanay; and her disappointment at missing the parties in town had been growing all evening. Now she wanted to leap at the chance to go, but restrained herself. It wouldn't do to appear too eager.

"It might be interesting after all," she said lightly. "Do you think they'd mind?" She motioned toward the chatting women.

"I'll fix it up while you get ready," Andy told her.

He came back as she finished pulling on her boots. "They're just getting warmed up," he reported. "They have a lot of catching up to do because they haven't been together for a while. Probably take them most of the night to get talked out."

April showed Mrs. Fergusson her new scarf before putting it on, and her aunts beamed.

"I'm glad you wore it," Andy said as they ran down the snow-covered steps of the terrace. "Your aunts looked so pleased, they were ready to burst."

The air was clear and cold; and, for once, he was without his cap and scarf. April jokingly wound her present around his neck. "Now you look more like yourself," she laughed. "Do you know tonight's the first time I've ever seen all of your face?"

"Hope it isn't too much of a shock," he replied with a grin.

April giggled. He could be fun even if he did prefer animals to humans!

In the driveway stood Clyde, hitched to his unusual boxlike sled. "I made this to take Granny around in," he explained. "She doesn't fancy sitting astride my horse."

"Small wonder!" April said as he helped her in.

154

"That's the most monstrous animal I've ever seen."

Clyde moved unhurriedly, but with great strides of his powerful legs; and the box glided swiftly down the road, its lanterns making yellow pools in the snow. Andy's skill made handling the contraption on the slick surface look deceptively easy.

April sat beside him on the driver's seat, which was a board built into the front of the box—a hard contrast to the upholstered seat in Bobby's sled. But she didn't mind. The owner of the board was taking her into town while the master of the comfortable sleigh had left her stranded.

The wind suddenly whipped the strong scent of skunk toward them, stinging their eyes.

"Whew!" April exclaimed. "Your friend Chanel's awfully generous with her perfume tonight!"

"Something's disturbed her, or one of her relatives. Must be a newcomer in the neighborhood. The regular residents usually leave them alone. I almost never smell them around here."

He seemed puzzled, and she was afraid he was going to stop to investigate. But he kept going. "Whatever was on the receiving end of that spray is gone by now," he said. "A lot sadder and maybe a little wiser."

They rode on a short distance, and Clyde came to an unexpected halt. A mass of rocks and snow barred the way. April was certain this was the same spot where she had deceived herself into making a wrong turn on her fateful trip up the road yesterday.

"Rock slide," Andy muttered as he fumbled in the bottom of the box for a shovel. "Happens all the time just because the road builders tried to save a few cents. Instead of following the contour of the mountain, they made the road straight right here. Gets blocked whenever we have a heavy rain or snow."

He used the shovel to push rocks and chunks of snow to the side of the road and quickly made enough room for the horse to get through.

"Probably be more here by the time we get back," he predicted and stowed the shovel in the sleigh.

The skunk odor was especially strong at this spot and reminded April of something she had been intending to ask: "How'd you get so interested in skunks and birds and other creatures?"

"My grandfather's responsible for that, I guess," Andy said. "We used to live in Scranton when I was growing up, but I spent Christmas and summer vacations here on the farm. Grandpa loved the out-of-doors, couldn't stand being cooped up. And I'm the same way. He seemed to have a special understanding of nature. People often get that way when they spend a lot of time in the fields.

156

"He and a forest ranger, Mr. McCleary over in Big Gap, were good friends; and the ranger got him interested in bird banding. So Grandpa taught me. We both banded under Mr. McCleary's license—and I still do."

"You have to have a license to band birds?" April asked, surprised.

"Sure! The Fish and Wildlife Service couldn't allow just anyone to trap birds. You have to qualify, be able to identify birds and keep careful records, that sort of thing. I'm going to try to get my own permit before long."

"Your grandfather must have been as much of a puzzle to the local people as my aunts are."

Andy gave a short laugh. "Yeah! Even his own relatives thought he was a little batty. They couldn't understand why he didn't work in the mines like the rest of them, instead of trying to scratch a living out of these hillsides. Of course Granny never doubted that he'd make a go of it, but it was pretty rough for them until Grandpa decided that apple trees should like these slopes. He did right well after that."

"My dad's people were all miners," April said, pleased that they had this in common. "All except my father. He wanted no part of mining."

"Mining's a strange business," Andy mused. "My father said mining would be the death

157

of him—and it was eventually—but he never quit. It seems to get hold of a man and won't turn him loose. He has to keep on mining whether he wants to or not."

"Creepy, isn't it?" April shuddered involuntarily. "I suppose that's why my grandfather found it so hard to understand why my father didn't want to go into the family mine."

"Good thing he didn't. He might have been caught in the big cave-in they had before the mine closed. Took a lot of lives, according to Granny."

"I didn't know about that," April said with interest. "No one told me."

"I shouldn't have, either," Andy said quickly. "I wasn't thinking. Your aunts wouldn't want that aired again. You won't mention it, will you?"

"But why wouldn't they want me to know about the cave-in?"

"Well, this was when Miss Elsbeth was secretly meeting her fiance, Jock Cameron, near the mine; and the rumor went around that she had actually been inside."

"What difference would that have made?"

"Miners are very superstitious. It's considered bad luck for a woman to go into the mines, so it wasn't hard for people to believe there was a connection between the cave-in and the story that a woman had broken tradition by entering the mine."

158

"That's crazy! Actually crazy!" April exclaimed. "And poor Aunt Elsbeth! No wonder my aunts stayed away from Glen Ayr if people were blaming Aunt Elsbeth for a mine accident. Do you think she really did go into the mine?"

"Nope. Not a word of truth to it. The rumor was started on purpose. Of course I don't believe it would've caused a cave-in even if she had gone in. But she didn't. Granny says so, and she oughta know because Jock Cameron was her brother."

"She told me that. But what happened to him?"

"He went back to the family home in Scranton after he lost his job here. He was going to try to get a job in the mines there so he and Miss Elsbeth could get married, but he caught cold and pneumonia developed. He died very suddenly. Too bad they didn't have antibiotics then."

"Too bad Aunt Elsbeth wasn't there. She might have fixed him up with some of her medicine. It's sad, isn't it, that they never married. I wonder who... What did you mean by 'the rumor was started on purpose'?"

"Did I say that?"

"You know very well you did. And I just remembered something else. Your grandmother said that it wasn't Mr. Cameron that Mrs. MacDonald was interested in, but my grandfather. She was young then and he was an old man. Why would she want to marry him?"

159

"It probably seemed an easy way for her to get her hands on a lot of money. While Miss Elsbeth was mourning the death of Jock Cameron and Miss Milly was busy with her own social life, Mrs. Mac-Donald had plenty of time to work on Mr. Mac-Kenzie. He wasn't well, and she almost convinced him that she was the only person interested in his welfare. Your aunts finally woke up to what was happening and saw to it that Della MacDonald was kept too busy to spend much time with their father."

"I wonder what would have happened if she'd managed to marry my grandfather," April said.

"Your aunts wouldn't be living in the Castle now," Andy said positively. "She would have thrown them out long ago."

"From what I hear, she's still trying." She hesitated, uncertain whether to tell him about her plan. Finally she said, "I thought I'd ask Bobby to put in a good word with his father. You know, about the taxes. But I haven't had a chance . . ."

Andy glanced at her and said a little too quickly, "I wouldn't do that. It could make things worse."

She should have known he would say something like that. He had made it plain enough last night that he didn't like Bobby. Of course she wasn't feeling too kindly toward Bobby herself, but she was sure he had a good reason for standing her up this evening.

160

"Glen Ayr isn't like most towns," Andy went on. "People don't come and go very much; they stay put. Things are changing a little now, but most of the older people have spent their entire lives here; and everybody knows everything about everybody else, including rumors. That's why it's hard to change their ideas. Time doesn't make them forget; it makes them remember. And you must admit that two women living in a castle on a mountaintop are natural targets for superstitious tales."

"I know," April said quietly, thinking of her own suspicions. "When you see a spooky castle, you automatically expect spooky people to be living there. I guess you see what you expect to see. But I don't know how I could have thought my aunts were anything but nice old ladies." She paused, then added, "And I'll bet a lot of the townspeople think they're okay. One of these days they'll speak up, and that will put the troublemakers out of business."

Andy threw back his head and laughed. "And everyone will live happily ever after," he teased. "Don't tell me you still believe in fairy tales?"

"I suppose I do, in a way. Oh, I don't believe ugly frogs always turn into handsome princes. They could just as easily turn into ugly princes. And I don't believe that wicked witches always melt or get burned up. Some of them must turn into math

161

teachers. But I really do believe that the good guys win sooner or later."

Andy laughed again. "Well, Snow White, who am I to say you're wrong?" He pulled on the reins and stopped in front of the post office.

The town was ablaze with light; and Main Street, usually deserted at dusk, was busier than on Saturday afternoons. There were crowds of people everywhere.

"It's the Daft Days for sure!" said Andy.

# CHAPTER

# 14

He saddled, he bridled,
   and gallant rode he,
And hame cam his gude horse,
   but never cam he.

*Old Scottish Ballad*

"WHERE TO FIRST?" Andy asked April as he tied Clyde to an old hitching post in front of the post office.

"Mr. and Mrs. Roberts asked me to stop by. Maybe we can work our way around from there."

"Suits me," Andy said. "I hope we run across Mr. McPherson. He gives me a hand sometimes, and I want to see if he'll help cover that mine shaft. It's a bigger job than I thought."

"Is it still open?"

"Oh, I put some planks over it to keep animals

163

out, but I wouldn't advise you to test it. By the way, the biggest celebration will be at the mayor's house. Are you game to go?"

"Yes!" she said firmly. She wanted to show Bobby Ramsay that she didn't need him to get into town. And she was also curious to know why he hadn't come for her.

They were swept along by a crowd of merry revelers and added their voices to the cries of "Happy New Year!" It was impossible not to be infected with the gaiety and lightheartedness that had taken over the town. Bagpipes wailed a lively tune while first-footers, many in kilts and tartans, danced a Scottish reel in the middle of the street. Others carried hot kettles of special holiday drink that they gave out or exchanged with friends on every corner. There was no doubt about it, everyone had gone a little mad.

"No wonder they're so quiet all the time," April said, standing on tiptoe at Andy's ear so she could be heard above the din. "They save their energy so they can explode at Hogmanay!"

The little living room of the Robertses' house was packed with well-wishers. Mr. Roberts, a dish in each hand, made his way toward them as they entered.

"Happy New Year!" he called. "The missus and I were wondering if you'd be down. She's in the kitchen—be right out. And how are you, Andy, my boy?" He put down the dishes, shook Andy's hand, then led them to a table laden with food.

"I promised April the best Pitcaithly bannocks in town, and here they are." He held out a plate of beautifully decorated shortbread. "My missus outdid herself this year," he stated with pride.

"I hardly know which one to take," April said, looking over the array. Each bannock was brightly colored and bore a message. She picked one with "A Merrie Auld Yule" written in red icing.

"Wonderful!" she said after a bite.

Mr. Roberts smiled broadly. "Have another," he urged before leaving to greet some new arrivals.

"I've never seen so much food!" she said to Andy, who was busily disposing of a plateful.

"Wait until you see the mayor's spread. Mrs. Ramsay thinks it's her civic duty to outdo everyone else, which suits me fine. I won't need to eat for a week."

"Or maybe a month," April told him as he sampled more of Mrs. Roberts's baking.

"Well, hello!" someone called in a voice meant to be seductive, but succeeded only in being hoarsely baritone. It was Virginia. "You ought to come into town more often. You're practically a stranger," she said, sidling up to Andy.

After much smiling and batting of eyelids, she

finally turned to April and asked in a patronizing tone, "Where's our little friend, Lot? I haven't seen him." She glanced around at the gathering of guests.

"Is he supposed to be here?" April wanted to know.

Virginia looked puzzled. "Well, since he brought you, I thought he'd be with you." She looked back at Andy and smiled encouragingly. There wasn't anything subtle about Virginia or her unspoken message for April to get lost.

April ignored it. "I didn't come with Lot and I haven't seen him. What made you think he'd brought me?"

"He and Bobby were discussing it on the way home last night—after that wild ride down the hill. It's lucky we weren't all killed!" She became indignant just thinking about it.

"Anyway, Ellen reminded Bobby that he'd promised to help his mother get things ready for the Eve, so then Lot said he'd come after you. He got real mad when Bobby decided not to come. First time he's ever stood up to anybody." She shook her head in disbelief.

"But he didn't come," April said. "Andy brought me."

Virginia's smile faded. "Maybe I misunderstood." She shrugged and drifted toward a group of noisy newcomers.

Andy and April said good-bye to the Robertses and moved on. In every house they visited, there was a great outlay of food. Money was obviously scarce in many places, but the people had somehow managed a tasty spread. And pastries and cakes were abundant.

"Scotland is sometimes called the Land o' Cakes," Andy reminded her. "All Scottish women worth their salt know how to bake." He gave her a wry grin.

"I'm only half Scottish. That's why my cooking's half-baked," she said, and they both laughed.

They were in high spirits when they approached the mayor's house. They had left this big celebration until last. April had resolved to be cool to Bobby until he apologized for breaking their date. But now she wasn't sure she could remain immune to his charm or whatever it was that sent her pulse racing every time she thought of him. She would probably turn to putty the minute he looked at her. But she didn't have to face Bobby just yet because he wasn't home when they arrived. He was visiting other parties.

As Andy had predicted, the refreshments at the mayor's surpassed all the others. April had never seen anything like it: hams, turkeys, chickens, cakes, and breads were spread out in abundance on the tables. The repasts at the other houses seemed meager by comparison. She wished she

167

had room to eat more, particularly after she had tasted such delicacies as rich, black rye loaves filled with fruit and peel; and something called a Scotch bun, with a lovely brown crust that was discarded, oddly enough, and only the filling eaten. This was made entirely of eggs, chopped fruit, and peel—or so Mrs. Ramsay informed her as she hovered about, keeping track of everybody and everything.

Andy had gone off to talk to Mr. McPherson about the mine covering when April spotted Mrs. MacDonald on a nearby window seat. She remembered that grievances were supposed to be put away during Hogmanay, so she strolled over to where Mrs. MacDonald sat and was greeted with the same hostile expression she had met on her arrival.

"Oh, it's you," Mrs. MacDonald replied when April said hello. "Thought you might be gone back to California by now. You're braver than most, staying this long up there."

"It's really very nice," April said innocently and saw the woman give her a sharp glance. "I understand you used to work at Greystone. The place didn't scare you, did it?"

"Greystone!" Mrs. MacDonald snorted. "It's 'Witches' Castle'! But folks up there weren't quite so batty when I worked . . ."

April suddenly noticed the cameo brooch she was wearing. It was a twin to Aunt Milly's!

168

At that moment, Bobby came in, along with more visitors who had made this their last stop and high point of the first-footing. As he greeted April, Mrs. MacDonald lost no time in joining another group. And she looked upset, April noted.

Bobby guided her to a quiet corner. "I'm terribly sorry about not coming for you," he said earnestly. "But I promised Mother to help set up things for the Eve. She would have been fit to be tied if I hadn't been here. You know how it is . . ."

He smiled that special smile of his and she melted. Yes, she knew how it was. Not only did his explanation seem logical, but she almost wanted to apologize for having expected him.

"And Lot insisted on coming," he went on, "so I knew you'd get here all right. By the way, where's Lot? Haven't seen him around all evening."

"I don't know," April said. "I came with Andy, not Lot."

Bobby looked worried. "It isn't like him to go back on a promise."

"Maybe he got sick," April suggested.

"He'd have let me know for sure. But there's his mother. We can ask her."

Before they could cross the room, a thin woman with the cares and worries of half a lifetime etched upon her face, hurried over to them.

169

"Nary a sign of him all this time," she began without preamble. "And where would he be keeping himself at Hogmanay?"

"I really don't know, but he'll probably be along soon. Must be at one of the parties. By the way, this is April MacKenzie." Bobby nodded toward the woman and murmured, "Mrs. Murphy, Lot's mother."

Mrs. Murphy looked her over carefully. "So you're the young lady from the hill? Well, you look all right to me," she announced.

April was glad of her approval, but she wondered what Mrs. Murphy had expected to see.

"Lot was going to bring April to town," Bobby told the woman. "I lent him my sleigh and Jezebel, but I guess he changed his mind because he didn't go after her."

"Didn't say a word to me or his pa about going up the hill. But then, he never does say much. Just keeps his head in a book all the time and doesn't know the time of day. Too much book reading's a worrisome thing." She stopped and stared at Bobby, some of the lines on her face deepening into a frown. "But your sleigh's in the driveway. And that speckly horse, too!"

"I'll have a look," said Bobby and rushed out with April at his heels. His piebald horse, reeking of skunk, was stamping impatiently in the lane that led to the stables, its way to a warm stall blocked by a jeep.

"That *is* Jezebel!" he exclaimed. "And she smells to high heaven! You didn't pass her on the way down, did you? No, you couldn't have; the road's too narrow."

He seemed to be talking more to himself than to her. He hesitated, then said, "You don't suppose . . . I mean, if Lot came to the Castle, you'd know it, wouldn't you?"

"Of course! He was coming for me, wasn't he?" She didn't see his point.

Bobby took a deep breath. "I guess you realize by now that some very odd things go on up there on the hill. And now with Lot missing, it looks as if people really do disappear. I know you aren't to blame, but . . ."

"But what?" she cried as anger struggled with fear for the upper hand.

"Well, can't you see? There has to be some reason why these things happen only up there. I mean, your aunts must have *something* to do with them."

She was angry now. "Maybe they turned Lot into a big, black bird," she said sarcastically. "Here you're accusing my aunts, and you don't know for sure that Lot's vanished. Or even if he started up the mountain."

"He came by for Jezebel and the sleigh at about nine o'clock. Said he was going up to get you, and no one's seen him since. The facts speak for themselves."

"I've been with my aunts all evening, and I know that Lot didn't come to the Castle. So if he's gone, they had nothing to do with it. You don't really believe they're witches, do you?"

"You don't have to be a witch to be wacky," Bobby cut in. "Everybody's known for a long time that your aunts weren't quite ... well, normal. They don't act like other people—you know that. And age doesn't usually make nutty people any saner, so they've probably reached the point where some of their crazy ideas have made them dangerous. You may be their niece, but you're taking a chance staying up there. One of these days they may forget you're related to them."

April stared at him in disbelief. "How can you say such a thing!" she cried finally. "You haven't seen my aunts for years—maybe you've never seen them. All you know about them is what people like Mrs. MacDonald and her daughter say and they're ... well, they're ..." She was so indignant, words refused to come. She had to fight to keep her emotions in check.

"Look, April," Bobby said, adopting a tone of quiet reason, "if you use your head, you can clear

172

up a messy situation. Why don't you persuade your aunts to sell the Castle for a fair price? You would all have a nice chunk of money."

April had an almost uncontrollable urge to slap Bobby's handsome face. He sounded like the wheeler-dealer Andy said he was. He wanted to help his mother and her scheming friends get her aunts' home.

"I . . . I can't believe it!" she sputtered. "You . . . you . . ."

"No use getting riled up," Bobby said calmly. "There's nothing you can do!"

"Well, we'll see about that . . ."

Bobby shook his head. "Too bad you're not as smart as I thought you were, April." He turned back toward the house. "If Lot hasn't showed up, I'll have to organize a search party," he called over his shoulder.

April stood rooted to the spot as the gay holiday suddenly dissolved into a black nightmare. If something had actually happened to Lot, everyone would be only too eager to blame her aunts. They had heard so many wild tales about the Castle, they couldn't help suspecting the worst. But for Bobby to ask her to persuade her aunts to give up their home! She hadn't known the real Bobby at all.

Concern for Lot's safety quickly merged with her concern for her aunts. If something *had* happened

173

to Lot, it would be because of her, because he had tried to be her friend. She felt sick all over.

News of Lot's absence spread like wildfire as knots of erstwhile revelers gathered to discuss it. April told Andy about her conversation with Bobby, and he seemed worried. From a window in the mayor's house, they watched the crowd outside grow in size and sound when those who had celebrated a little too freely around the wassail bowl joined in.

"Let's go up there and settle this once and for all!" someone shouted.

The undercurrent of talk began to swell. The laughter and joking ended abruptly. The mood of the crowd changed ominously.

Andy took April's arm and drew her into the Ramsays' kitchen. "I don't like the looks of this," he whispered. "This mob may decide to go up the hill. We'd better get there first."

They slipped out the back door and worked their way along the edge of the milling crowd, hoping to reach the post office unnoticed.

Timid Mayor Ramsay was nervously urging everyone to remain calm while a search party was organized. But he couldn't silence the angry cries that were straining the tension and holding reason at bay.

"And what about that mine accident?" a shrill female voice cried.

174

"What about it?" a man called.

"It wasn't an accident!" the shrill voice declared and was followed by a chorus of "Aye!" "Right you are!"

Mrs. MacDonald was finally having her day.

# CHAPTER

# 15

Awa, awa, you ill woman,
  You've not come here for gude;
You're but a witch, or wile warlock,
  Or mermaid o' the flude.
                    *Old Scottish Ballad*

At Andy's urging, Clyde picked up his big feet
and moved rapidly up the mountain road. Light
snow had drifted back across the spot where they
had encountered the barrier on the way down, but
the horse moved through it easily.

"Do you think they'll come to the Castle?" April
asked, unnerved by the display of emotion she had
witnessed. "Some of them have had too much to
drink, and they're spoiling for a fight. No telling
what they'd do up here."

"I think they'll use up their energy searching for Lot. But warn your aunts to lock all the doors and not to open them for anyone."

"I was talking to Mrs. MacDonald tonight. She didn't seem too pleased to see me and..." April stopped, remembering the figure in the kitchen. "You know, Andy, just before you and your grandmother arrived, I caught a glimpse of someone sneaking out the kitchen door. Maybe it was a shadow—I was half-asleep so I can't be sure—but it looked like Mrs. MacDonald."

"Wouldn't be the first time Della MacDonald's been poking around the Castle," Andy said matter-of-factly.

"But—but I thought she was afraid. She's the one talking about witches all the time."

"That's for the benefit of the townspeople. She's afraid of Mad and Gabriel because they get after her, but that's all. I've caught her snooping around several times. And Ellen, too."

"Ellen! Why, she pretended to be scared to death coming up here!" April was surprised by this information. "I don't get it. What do they want? What are they looking for?"

"Maybe the same thing other people are looking for," Andy said. For a moment this made no sense to her; then it began to take on significance.

"You mean the same reason my aunts are knocking down the Castle walls?"

"Uh-huh. I've tried to get them to stop—one day they're going to bring the whole place down around their ears—but they keep at it. Fortunately it's unusually well built."

"That still doesn't tell me what they're looking for, or what Mrs. MacDonald wants, unless . . ." Then she remembered the brooch the woman had been wearing. Perhaps she had stolen it from Aunt Elsbeth. And she could have taken her mother's diamond ring, too. That would account for its sudden disappearance.

"Maybe Mrs. MacDonald's already found what she's looking for," April told him.

"I doubt it, or she wouldn't keep coming back. But it would be better if you waited for your aunts to explain about their search. I don't think they'd appreciate it if I told you. They may be hard up, but they have a lot of pride."

They had reached the driveway, and Andy helped her out of the sleigh. "I'll be back soon," he said. "I want to take a look at that old mine shaft. It's just a hunch—may not amount to anything."

"Oh, no! That could be where Lot is!" April exclaimed. "If he's been hurt trying to be nice to me . . ." Her voice trailed off.

Andy said reassuringly, "It's possible, you know, that he's still in town somewhere, that he decided not to come up here after all." He turned the horse and sleigh around and started back down the mountain.

In the great hall, the fire burned brightly on the hearth, yet only Mad, still perched on the mantel, enjoyed its warmth. Her aunts and Mrs. Fergusson weren't there.

"That's odd!" April said aloud.

She went into the kitchen, but they weren't there, either. Then she heard the familiar sound of hammers on stone. "They're at it again!" She was surprised that they would undertake this task with a guest present. They usually made quite a secret of their hobby.

"What a time for them to be hacking away at the walls!" April said as she went to the east wing where the noise seemed to originate. She opened the door to the first tower, and on the steps were Aunt Milly and Aunt Elsbeth, in smocks and dust-caps, and Andy's grandmother as well. They all stopped, hammers poised in midair, like three statues. Then with sheepish grins, they came to life.

"We didn't hear you come in." Aunt Milly was the first to speak.

"Just doing a little work while we waited," Aunt Elsbeth said casually, and they all nodded in agreement.

April stood her ground. She was determined to get to the bottom of this right now. "I know this is your home and you can do whatever you want with it, but something serious has come up. I think it'll help if we're all perfectly frank with each other. I know you're looking for something, but I don't know why you can't tell me about it."

The three of them exchanged questioning glances, and Aunt Elsbeth took the initiative. She laid down her hammer and came down the steps. "We should have told you from the beginning," she said quietly, "but we hoped and prayed that we'd find what we're looking for, and then we wouldn't have to tell you."

April looked bewildered. She understood less now than before.

"You see," Aunt Elsbeth explained, "we thought that if you knew just how bad off financially we are, you might not want to stay. We really have very little actual cash, and we can't give you much in the way of clothes or things that young girls enjoy. But at the same time, we don't want to lose you. You've no idea how much brighter our lives are now that you're here. It's like a breath of spring to have a young person around, particularly James's daughter." Aunt Elsbeth kept herself in tight control, but April noted the break in her voice.

Aunt Milly could remain silent no longer.

"We're sure, from some of the things Papa said, that he hid his money here someplace—maybe in the walls. He didn't spend it, that's certain! He was very close with money, Papa was. Yet when he died, we found only a hundred dollars or so in his strong box. He didn't trust banks, so unless he gave it . . ." She left the sentence unfinished and went on. "Papa was a little eccentric in his later years. Got all sorts of strange ideas. I'm not speaking ill of the dead, mind you," she hastened to add. "It wasn't his fault; it was just old age."

Now Mrs. Fergusson spoke up in her usual brusque manner, "This is a family matter and I shouldn't butt in, but that's never stopped me before!" She gave a loud laugh that resembled Mad's croak.

"Seriously, my dear, your aunts have been in a real dither over this money affair. I told them you didn't care whether you had a lot of finery—knew the minute I saw you you weren't the type to lay a lot of store on looks. Of course you'd like pretty clothes; what young girl wouldn't? But there are other things more important. And I'll bet dollars to doughnuts you'd make the right choice in a pinch.

"But Elsbeth and Milly didn't want to take a chance, so they've been trying desperately to find the money. Never cared before whether they

181

found it or not. Got along all right without it. Now they need it, so Andy's been helping them sell some of their antique furniture to raise cash. Since my rheumatism's better, I persuaded them to let me help look. I've got a pretty good nose for sniffing out things, and I thought it might work on money, too!"

April was astounded. She hadn't dreamed her aunts were doing all this for her sake—even selling the family heirlooms! That accounted for all the missing furniture. She felt unworthy and ashamed as she thought of her suspicions about these two when she first came. And Ellen's tale about her father hadn't helped.

"Didn't Grandfather MacKenzie think my father took his money?" she asked.

Her aunts looked at her blankly. "Where did you get such an idea?" Aunt Elsbeth exclaimed. "Why, James would never take a cent that didn't belong to him!"

Aunt Milly shook her head sadly. "I'm afraid someone's been filling you full of the nonsense that keeps circulating in town. It's true Papa accused Jim of taking his money, but he accused everybody at one time or another—even us! As I told you, he had some queer ideas when he was old; and he couldn't remember what he did with anything. The doctor said hardening of the arteries had affected his mind, poor soul! The last time Jim was

182

home, he and Papa had a row over the money. We tried to tell Jim that Papa didn't mean it, that he was sick, but your father said that he excited Papa just by being here. They never could agree on anything. So Jim left and didn't come back."

"Unfortunately," Aunt Elsbeth added, "Della MacDonald overheard that argument—she worked here then—and she spread her own version of it all over town. Poor woman! Greed can become a disease if you aren't careful."

Aunt Milly then picked up the story: "Of course we never let on to Jim that we didn't find the money. It would have worried him terribly. He assumed we were well fixed after Papa died. He may even have wondered why we didn't share the estate with him, but he never said anything."

April was relieved to get a plausible explanation for some of this mystery. "I—I don't know what to say," she stammered, then remembered the urgency of the moment. "Right now, there's something I must tell you. It can't wait."

The three women gathered around her, prepared for the worst. "Lot Murphy disappeared on his way up the mountain, and a search party's coming to look for him—a whole mob of people. Some of them seem to think that you might've had something to do with his disappearance. I don't know what they'll do. They're in an ugly mood."

Unexpectedly, Aunt Milly and Aunt Elsbeth

relaxed and smiled. "We thought at first it was more serious," Aunt Milly said. "Of course I'm sorry to hear that someone's missing; but as for the townspeople making trouble for us, don't worry about that. We're used to it. We know all about the stories they tell. No use denying them—that only makes things worse. We found that out long ago, didn't we, Elsbeth?"

The older sister nodded.

"But this *is* serious!" April broke in. "If they don't find Lot, why, they might do most anything! Some of them even blame you because they haven't seen a salesman who usually comes through here. So that makes it worse."

Her aunts refused to get upset. "The sheriff and some men came up here some time ago looking for an itinerant peddler. We hadn't seen him, and we told them so," Aunt Elsbeth said.

April knew that she might as well drop the subject, but she wished they understood how explosive this situation was.

The sisters and Mrs. Fergusson washed up in the kitchen and once more sat before the fire.

"Good gracious! Where's Andy?" his grandmother suddenly asked. "I'd almost forgotten him!"

"He'll be here in a few minutes," April said. "He's checking on something. I'll see if he's coming yet."

She left the hall, silently praying that Andy had found Lot—unharmed. To think, he'd been willing to come all the way up here by himself so she wouldn't miss the celebration! She fervently hoped she'd get the chance to thank Lot—in person.

April ran up the winding stairs and looked out a window at the end of the corridor. There no sign of Andy, but in the distance the sky was aglow with the orange flames of lanterns and torches and the white glare of flashlights. Then she saw a sight that sent chills down her spine. A sinister mass of black figures was moving along the mountain road, heading for the Castle.

As the silhouetted figures came closer, she could see that they weren't searching very far from the road. She thought that they probably had decided it was too dangerous to search the woods in the dark and they'd wait until dawn, which wouldn't be long in coming. There was already a flush of pink in the eastern sky.

The mob moved steadily forward. They weren't searching at all! They were coming toward the Castle, rapidly and purposefully. April ran back down the stairs to the great hall.

"They're coming!" she told the women. "A big crowd—right up the road!"

"Maybe you'd better come to my house," Granny suggested. "You can't reason with a mob like that, especially if some of them have been celebrating too much. By morning they'll cool off and wonder why they were up here, but they can cause a lot of trouble in the meantime."

"Nothing's been gained so far by running away. We should have faced up to this business long ago and tried to straighten it out," Aunt Elsbeth said firmly. "When feeling was running high over the mine accident and the sheriff warned us that there was danger, we should have gone right into town anyway. So this time we're not running."

She paused and turned to Mrs. Fergusson. "Thank you for your help, but now you'd better go. And will you take April with you? There's no point in either of you getting involved. My sister and I can handle it."

April thought they were being foolhardy, but she was proud of their courage.

"Now look here, Elsbeth," cried Granny in her foghornlike voice, "you can't send me along and then you stay and have all the fun! It isn't fair! You know very well I've been laying for Della Mac-Donald for months and she's always a jump ahead of me. But it would be just like her to show up here tonight, urging that crowd on and hoping it'll get out of hand, or my name's not Rumpelstilt-skin!"

They all laughed, and the tension broke.

"If you're not running, why should I?" April asked gently. "You're my family, so I'm staying, too."

Her aunts smiled before resuming their worried look. "Very well," said Aunt Elsbeth. "We may as well sit down and await whatever is going to happen."

The three women sat in front of the fire, while Mad perched on the mantel and Genevieve, who'd left the kitchen hearth, prowled back and forth, her tail twitching angrily.

April went back upstairs to check on the mob's progress. If only Andy were back! she thought. He'd know what to do. And if he found Lot, there would be no need for this search party that wasn't really searching.

Even before she reached a window, she could see the lights. The whole mountain top seemed as bright as day. The crowd had moved into the driveway, close enough for her to hear the crunch of snow and ice beneath its feet. She raced downstairs again, just in time to hear a gentle knock on the door.

A man's thick voice called out, "That's no way to knock on a castle door. You do it like this!" Boom, boom, boom—three loud raps echoed through the hall, sending the raucous Mad to a high rafter and Genevieve into a hissing fury.

"Step back, please. Make way." April recognized the meek voice of the mayor.

"Better watch the windows, Mayor. They'll come flying out," someone joked, drawing a loud laugh from the crowd.

Aunt Elsbeth and Aunt Milly put on their coats, and April did the same. But Granny was busy peering out the windows to see who was there.

"Ready?" asked Aunt Elsbeth, her hand on the ornate door latch.

They nodded. She raised the latch and, in one grand, defiant sweep, flung open the door.

# CHAPTER
# 16

I'm neither witch nor wile warlock,
  Nor mermaid o' the sea,
I'm but Fair Annie o' Roch Royal,
  O open the door to me.
                              *Old Scottish Ballad*

"GOOD-EVENING," said the mayor politely. "Or perhaps I should say, 'Good-morning'."

"For goodness sake, Arthur! Get on with it!" Mrs. Ramsay urged impatiently.

"Yeah! Tell Witch Hazel why we're here. Tell her," called the man who had done the knocking.

"We're looking for young Lot," Mayor Ramsay explained. "He seems to have disappeared, and we were wondering if you'd seen him. I understand he was to call for your niece this evening."

189

"I'm sorry, but he hasn't been here. We've seen no sign of him," said Aunt Elsbeth.

"Not a sign," added Aunt Milly.

"Let me handle this," Mrs. Ramsay said, moving her massive bulk forward. "Now, my dear ladies, we're very sorry to bother you at this hour," she began disarmingly, "but I want you to think back and try to remember exactly what happened this evening. It's very important because a boy's life may be at stake." She spoke to the sisters as if she were addressing two backward children.

Before she could continue, Aunt Elsbeth drew herself up with dignity and said, "As we just told your husband, we know nothing about the boy. Of course we're very sorry that he's missing, but we have no idea where he is. He could have strayed off the road, so perhaps if you searched for him . . ."

"We *have* searched," replied Mrs. Ramsay. "That's why we've come here—quite peacefully— to ask your help, to be sure nothing has slipped your mind. We know that the boy was at least halfway here because we found his cap on the road."

April recognized the cap she held out as the one Lot usually wore. She prayed once again that he was safe and that Andy would find him. Mrs. Ramsay's insinuations were making her aunts appear senile and incompetent. But perhaps that was the whole idea.

"And what about that missing peddler?" someone

in the crowd called. "Did he come up here and disappear, too?"

"Yeah! What about it?" cried the thick-voiced man who had knocked on the door. "We should do something about this! Everybody's disappearing."

"You don't mind if we take a look around, do you?" asked Mrs. Ramsay.

Aunt Milly glanced at her sister, waiting for her to make the decision. Aunt Elsbeth hesitated, then started to speak, "We think . . ."

A sudden, loud screeching from inside the Castle interrupted her. The noise at first sounded like a cat fight, but as it drew closer, words were distinguishable—high-pitched and angry.

"Come along, now, and stop all that caterwauling," Granny boomed, but the shrieking continued. Then Granny appeared in the doorway, holding a squirming Mrs. MacDonald.

"I'm not as spry as I once was," Granny announced, "but I can move fast enough to catch a thief."

"Who are you calling a thief?" cried Mrs. MacDonald, trying to free herself from Mrs. Fergusson's grip.

"You! That's who!" exclaimed Granny. "Found her sneaking around in the kitchen while everyone was out front. Now then, what have you got to say about that? And it isn't the first time you've been up here. I saw you myself once."

191

"I don't know what you're talking about!" Mrs. MacDonald shrilled. "And take your hands off me!"

The crowd gaped at this unusual sight, and no one moved to interfere.

"Not until you tell them how come you're always scaring people with talk about witches and black magic, but it doesn't scare you. How come?"

"I'm going to have the law on you! You see her, don't you," Mrs. MacDonald cried, addressing the crowd. "Assaulting me, that's what she's doing!"

"I'm holding a criminal for sneaking into somebody's house. No telling what you were up to . . ."

Mrs. MacDonald's coat had come open as she tried to escape Granny's hold, and now the cameo brooch was in full view.

"Ah, ha! Now look there!" Granny pounced. "There's only two of those brooches in existence. Mr. Kirkland in Baltimore copied one from the other. No trouble to prove that. Now, there's one," she pointed to the brooch Millicent MacKenzie was wearing, "and there's its mate—been missing for years." She shoved a finger toward the pin Mrs. MacDonald wore on her dress. "Is that more black magic, or is it burglary?"

"No such thing!" exclaimed Mrs. MacDonald, on the defensive. "This brooch was a gift. A perfectly honest gift!"

"Ah, ha!" Granny cried again. "If that's true,

then you won't mind saying who gave it to you. It wasn't my brother, Jock, I know, although you've led people to believe you were stuck on him. So who was it?"

"None of your business!"

"Well, maybe the sheriff will make it his business to tuck you away for stealing."

"It was from Sam MacKenzie, if you must know," blurted Della MacDonald. "And it was a gift—for good work!"

There was a moment of silence, then Granny released the weasel-faced woman, who darted back into the mob. "Just wanted to hear you admit what the real situation was, Della," she said. "I've been saying all along that you had old Sam wrapped around your finger after his mind got fuzzy. And you almost married him! If your plan had worked out, you would be mistress of Greystone now. Folks should take that into account when you talk. Puts all your tales in a different light. Maybe now they won't be so ready to put stock in them."

A muttering ran through the crowd as this information sank in.

Mrs. Ramsay spoke up quickly, before emotions could cool and this unique opportunity be lost. "Mrs. Fergusson, your feud with Della MacDonald isn't helping us find Lot. We'd better get on with the search without wasting any more time."

193

"Hold on!" Granny shouted. She turned to the mayor. "Are you going to permit a search—right in your official presence—without a proper search warrant?"

"Come, now!" Mrs. Ramsay broke in. "There's nothing official about this. It's simply a matter of cooperation. Someone's lost and we want to find him. I'm sure the MacKenzie sisters won't mind."

"Now look here, Agatha Ramsay, I was talking to His Honor, the Mayor," said Mrs. Fergusson. "But I might as well straighten you out first. Everybody knows about your little scheme. You may call it 'community relations,' or whatever you want, but taking over people's homes isn't right. That's all there is to it! And it's time some of our so-called solid citizens took a stand on this business. So I'm saying for the record, that if you, *Mr.* Mayor, let the taxes on this property get jacked up dishonestly, I'll use the bit I have laid by, to help the Mac-Kenzies fight you in court."

The mayor cleared his throat uncertainly, but Mrs. Ramsay didn't hesitate. "The very idea!" she cried, "suggesting the mayor would go along with anything dishonest. He won't reply to such insolence!"

To everyone's surprise, including his wife's, Mr. Ramsay stepped forward and said firmly, "The mayor *will* reply. The taxes on this property, or

194

any other property in Glen Ayr, will be completely fair, I'll see to that!"

The crowd responded with applause, and the mayor looked around, pleased with this reception.

"We must get on with the search," Mrs. Ramsay said irritably.

"Be quiet, Agatha. I'll handle this." Apparently the applause had gone to the mayor's head because he had never before opposed her in public. While Mrs. Ramsay stared, dumbfounded, he squared his shoulders and went on. "Now about the search . . ."

"It's all right," Aunt Elsbeth interrupted. "They can search if they want to. We have nothing to hide . . ."

At that moment, the clip-clop of horses' feet diverted the attention of the crowd, and a sleigh pulled into the driveway. It was Andy's. April recognized its angular appearance even in the dim light of dawn. But only one figure sat on the board seat. Her heart sank.

Almost immediately, another sleigh followed the first. This one belonged to Mr. Roberts. He and Andy were lifting someone from the bottom of the box sleigh.

A cold chill enveloped her as one thought burned in her mind: Lot is dead!

# CHAPTER

# 17

And for auld lang syne, my jo,
   For auld lang syne,
We'll tak a cup o' kindness yet,
   For auld lang syne.

*Robert Burns*

APRIL TURNED AWAY quickly, unwilling to witness more sadness on this day that should have been the gayest of the year.

"Andy found him in an open mine shaft," April heard Mr. Roberts say.

"It's just my ankle," a familiar voice was explaining.

April forced herself to look back. There, standing between Mr. Roberts and Andy, and leaning on them for support, was Lot, talking to his mother. April couldn't believe her eyes. Relief overwhelmed her, and she brushed away the tears that ran down her cheeks.

"Bring him in here," someone ordered quietly. All eyes turned toward the Castle where Elsbeth and Millicent MacKenzie still stood in the great, arched doorway. Only now, Genevieve peered cautiously from behind their skirts.

"Bring him in here," Aunt Elsbeth repeated. "He must be frozen." She started to say something else, changed her mind, then began again. "If the rest of you would like a drop of punch and would like to warm up by the fire, we would be pleased to have you come in." She turned and marched into the Castle.

April went up to Lot as Andy and Mr. Roberts helped him inside. "I'm so sorry, Lot. How did it happen?"

Lot sat down and gave her a weak smile. "Darndest thing! The horse stopped because a rock slide had blocked the road. And just as I was getting out to take a look, a skunk let loose—must have been cornered in front of the roadblock. Anyway, Jezebel reared up and dumped me in the snow, then took off. I went after her; and all of a sudden, there I was, falling to China—except something broke my fall and kept me from going all the way down. Jezebel veered off into the woods and missed the hole, luckily. Bobby would have taken me apart if anything had happened to her."

197

"I'm so sorry!" April said again. "And thanks for trying to come for me. I'll never forget that." She wanted to hug him but felt he might not understand.

Lot looked at her shyly. "Wasn't anything. I just didn't want you to be disappointed." He hesitated, wincing as he shifted position. "You've been nicer to me than anybody. A real friend."

She detected a slight emphasis on the word "friend" and glanced at him quickly. Their eyes met; and she knew, instinctively, that he did understand. She leaned over and kissed him gently on the cheek.

With darting looks and shuffling feet, the crowd outside fidgeted uncomfortably, trying to decide whether to accept Miss MacKenzie's invitation. In the cold light of day and now that the fortifying effects of the celebration had worn off, things looked different. Most of them seemed less than happy about their performance here.

"You are a troublemaker, Della MacDonald!" Mrs. Murphy's voice rang out. She stood in the doorway, calling after a form retreating down the hill. "I'm ashamed of listening to you at all!"

The others nodded in agreement and promptly laid their feelings of guilt on the hapless Mrs. MacDonald. With that settled, they swarmed into the Castle for a cup of warm punch.

198

The lavish baking had been providential; there was food and drink for everyone. And for the first time in many years, the great hall was filled with guests.

At the first opportunity, Mr. Roberts spoke quietly with the sisters. "I started up the hill as soon as I heard about the trouble, but I stopped to look around when I saw that light in the woods. Struck me as mighty unusual. Of course it turned out to be Andy's lantern." He studied his feet. "I believe I owe you an apology even though I didn't take part in what went on up here. It's easy to be a sheep—follow right along when you ought to be breaking new trail. I've been a poor neighbor, I'm afraid, but maybe it's not too late to make amends."

"Nonsense!" Aunt Milly said. "You have certainly gone out of your way to be nice to April. Besides we haven't been very neighborly ourselves. Perhaps this little affair tonight has a bright side. It may clear the air of a lot of things."

After Aunt Elsbeth slipped a bit of one of her herb brews into Lot's cup of punch, his color improved and his ankle pained him less.

"I feel fine! No point in seeing a doctor now," he protested.

"We're going to take you to Dr. Hanson anyway," said his uncle, a tall, muscular man, who picked him up and carried him to Mr. Roberts's sleigh.

"I'll be back to see you again," Lot promised April as he left. "And next time I'll make it all the way up the hill!"

The townspeople ate and drank and enjoyed the warmth of the fire, all the while looking around the great hall with open curiosity. They seemed to find it more interesting than frightening—even when Mad stole a raisin cake right off the plate of the loudmouthed man who had banged on the door. Now he laughed uproariously and tempted the bird to perform again.

April noted that neither Mrs. Ramsay nor Bobby was present. But the mayor, thoroughly enjoying his new role, was self-appointed master of ceremonies for the occasion. After a suitable interval, he rose and thanked the MacKenzies for their hospitality, particularly under the circumstances. And he urged them to come into town where, he assured them, a warm welcome awaited. There was a polite murmuring of thanks from the unexpected guests. Then they were gone.

In the empty hall April's aunts and Mrs. Fergusson sank into chairs by the fire and sipped tea and Aunt Elsbeth's tonic to calm their nerves.

"We've never had a Hogmanay like this! Not ever!" Aunt Milly announced, still slightly dazed by it all.

"It's just as well," said Aunt Elsbeth. "I don't think I could stand more than one."

Granny, for once, said nothing.

April and Andy cleared away the remains of the party and began washing dishes while the ladies recovered. As they worked in the quiet kitchen, the turmoil of the past few hours seemed far away. April found it hard to convince herself that just a short time ago the Castle had been filled with people, and before that . . .

"Wasn't this the wildest night, ever?" she asked Andy.

"Barbarians!" he muttered for the fifth time. "They lose all reason when they get in packs!" He was still shaken by the sight that had greeted him when he brought Lot back—the mob confronting four women.

"It's all over now," April soothed. "And maybe some good will come out of it. I think the townspeople will be nicer to my aunts now that they know these tales about them aren't true."

"I wouldn't count on it," said Andy. "They won't give up such a topic for gossip that easily."

"Well, I must admit that it isn't every town that has nice old ladies in a castle with ravens and roosters and heaven-knows-what-else for pets, and a jungle of plants, and who make their own medicine. I mean, it would be kind of hard not to talk about them. But if people visit here . . . Hey, that reminds me. Did you know that Mrs. MacDonald sneaked in here while the crowd was out front? Granny caught her." She described the scene, and Andy rocked with laughter.

"But what could she be after?" April asked, becoming serious.

"I think she believes, just as your aunts do, that your grandfather hid some money here. She may even have convinced herself that she has a right to it. That's why she's anxious to get rid of your aunts, so they won't find it first. I imagine she keeps check on their progress whenever she's up here."

"But why would she spread that tale about my aunts stealing the money and blaming it on my father—then pretending there wasn't any for the pension fund? That doesn't make sense."

"Don't underestimate Mrs. MacDonald," Andy told her. "That was a sure way to turn the townspeople against your aunts. The miners' pension fund affects almost every family, and when the people thought your aunts were holding out on them, naturally they became bitter. Besides, remember that many of them believed your Aunt Elsbeth was the cause of the mine cave-in."

"I don't see how Mrs. MacDonald can be so mean!" April moaned. "And all those tales about witches!"

"It's probably been a very satisfactory revenge from her point of view," Andy said. "Don't forget, she would have owned the Castle now if your aunts hadn't interfered. And to be perfectly fair, she didn't invent much of that witch business. People have always been superstitious about this place. She and Ellen just embroidered the stories and kept them going. They served to keep the curious from nosing around up here and getting in their way."

April was silent for a minute. Then she asked hesitantly, "Do you think Mrs. Ramsay—and Bobby —were in on it? Deliberately trying to force my aunts out?"

Andy was thoughtful. "No, I think Mrs. Ramsay has a knack of convincing herself that she's interested only in doing good. Of course what she thinks is good for others, usually works out to be good for Agatha Ramsay. But I don't think she intends to be malicious—like Mrs. MacDonald, who makes no bones about being mean. As for Bobby, well, he's interested mainly in Bobby." Andy looked at her sympathetically. "I'm sorry to be so blunt, but you asked."

"It's all right. I know it's true; I was just wondering . . ." She took a deep breath and switched topics. "From now on things are going to be different around here. I'm going to see that my aunts get a new image, only I'm not sure yet how I'm going to do it. Maybe have more communication between the Castle and Glen Ayr . . . sort of bring the mountain to the town," she finished with a grin. "Will you come with me sometimes?"

"Wait a minute! You're the public relations agency," Andy began, then softened when he saw her disappointment. "Well, maybe. It's just that I don't have as much faith in my fellow men as you have. Now if we were dealing with foxes or skunks, I'd know how they'd react. But with people, I'm never sure."

"I think some of the townspeople will start coming up here now. Mr. Roberts, for instance, and the mayor—if his wife doesn't get the upper hand again."

They both laughed. "He probably will want to return to the scene of his victory," Andy agreed.

"And if my aunts visit in Glen Ayr, people will get to know them—see that they're plain human beings."

The dishes were finally finished, and they sat down before the big kitchen hearth.

"I don't think people change like that," Andy replied. "But I hope you prove I'm wrong."

"I do, too. My aunts deserve a break. Imagine, selling their lovely things just to get money for me! If I could find my mother's diamond ring, I'd sell it and get money for *them*."

"Where did you lose it?" Andy asked quickly.

"I didn't. It was right on the dresser in my room and just vanished. I thought Mrs. MacDonald . . ."

Andy leaned forward, his eyes sparkling. "Did you notice anything on your dresser that hadn't been there before the ring disappeared?"

April thought a minute. "No. Why?" His intense interest puzzled her.

"There was nothing different?" he persisted.

"Well, there was an old acorn."

"Aha!" Andy cried triumphantly. "I thought so! Raffles has been up to his old tricks again."

"Raffles? My aunts mentioned that name."

"A brown creature about so big." Andy held his hands approximately nine inches apart. "Has white feet, and he's not very sociable."

"More animals!" April muttered. "Say! Does this one look like a rat with a fuzzy tail and kind of big ears?"

"Raffles does look like a rat, which isn't too unusual since he is one. He's a pack rat or woods rat. They're thieves, but they're nice about it. They always leave something in exchange for whatever they borrow—a pine cone, stick, or something. That acorn on your dresser was a clue. Points right to Raffles."

"But what would he want with my ring? He can't eat it."

"Pack rats have a weakness for bright things, especially anything that glitters. Your ring would be irresistible to him. Miss Milly had some spoons missing several months ago, so I checked around and found Raffles's nest. Sure enough, he had the spoons hidden away."

April listened in wonder. "Does he actually give something in return for what he takes?" She suspected Andy was teasing her.

"So help me! But I doubt if a pack rat knows that he's doing it. You see, they're always carrying something in their mouths—it's second nature with them. So when they see something they like, particularly something shiny, they drop whatever they're carrying, because they can hold only one thing at a time, and pick up the new object. That's why people think they're 'honest thieves.'"

"If we can find Raffles's nest, maybe we can find my ring," April said excitedly. "What are we waiting for?"

Andy laughed. "Not so fast. First of all, where did you see Raffles last? I'm sure he has a new nest by now because I had to tear up his old one to retrieve the spoons."

"He was headed toward the east wing." She stood up. "I don't feel the least bit sleepy. I guess I've got my second wind. How about you?"

"I'm all right now, although I was pretty beat after getting Lot out of that shaft. But I'm sure

206

Granny wants to get home. She and your aunts must be exhausted. Suppose I come back this evening and help you look?"

They left the kitchen and approached the great hall. Everything was unusually quiet; they could hear no voices. Andy hurried forward to see what was wrong. The three ladies still sat before the dying fire, and all three were sound asleep. April smiled at the peaceful sight. It would be a shame to awaken them. Andy tiptoed to the hearth and placed another log on the fire, then picked up the kerosene lamp and beckoned her to follow.

The sun was up and shining brightly, but when they entered the gloomy darkness of the tower, she understood why he had brought the lamp. As they ascended the steps, Andy stopped every few feet to check the circular walls. Here and there stones had been pried out and inexpertly shoved back.

"If your aunts don't quit loosening these stones, the whole tower's going to fall down."

"Maybe we should watch Mrs. MacDonald when she comes up here and find out which part of the Castle she's interested in."

"Watch out!" Andy called. "They've left some tools here on the floor."

They had reached the platform at the top of the tower. It seemed to be a storage area—full of old trunks and boxes.

"Maybe the nest is behind some of this junk," April suggested, but Andy continued to look above him.

"These fellows build their nests on cliffs and although Raffles prefers to live in the Castle, I doubt if he can ignore his instincts."

Holding the lamp over his head, he turned slowly around. He had almost made a complete circle when he stopped abruptly.

"Look up there," he said and pointed.

She followed the direction of his finger and saw a great bundle of trash piled on the ledge below one of the windows. "That's just rubbish that's collected there."

"It's rubbish, all right," Andy agreed. "Just the kind of rubbish pack rats love. Take the lamp and watch."

With ease, he climbed the jutting stones that formed footholds to the ledge and began removing sticks, acorns, paper, tinfoil—an endless variety of trash—from the bundle. Raffles wasn't home.

"He's probably out collecting more treasures," Andy said as he dug farther into the pile. "Look at this!" He tossed her an object. It was a bar of soap.

"Uh, oh! More spoons." He threw down two of her aunts' silver spoons. "I guess Miss Milly hasn't missed those yet."

Now he began a more thorough search of the nest, carefully pulling apart the tightly packed stuff. After a few minutes, he spoke; and her heart leaped at the excitement in his voice. "It's here! I have it!"

Andy scampered down the stones to the platform and placed the diamond ring in the palm of her hand. There it glowed in the lamplight like a bit of cold fire.

"I thought I'd never see it again!" she whispered. "And if you didn't know so much about animals, it would have stayed there forever."

Andy looked embarrassed. "It's beautiful!" he said. "I'll bet your aunts won't want you to sell it."

"They won't know about it. It would only make them feel bad." She shivered, suddenly mindful of the cold dampness of the tower.

"We'd better get out of here before we both freeze," Andy said.

As he turned to go, his shoe caught on the corner of one of the many boxes. He stumbled and plunged forward—toward the steep, stone steps.

# CHAPTER

# 18

Here's to the friends we can trust
  When storms of adversity blaw;
May they live in our songs and be nearest
      our hearts,
  Nor depart like the year that's awa'.

*John Dunlop*

APRIL WATCHED HELPLESSLY as Andy dived toward the long stairs. At the last moment, he flung out his hands, caught one of the protruding stones, and steadied himself.

"Whew! That was close," he gasped, staring into the darkness below.

April sank down on one of the trunks, too weak

to say anything. In a moment Andy came back to the offending box that had turned over, spilling its contents across the floor.

"Must be old business records for the mine," he said, picking up ledgers and account books. "Your aunts say Mr. MacKenzie never threw anything away." He got down on his knees and peered beneath an old desk. "Saw something roll under here."

April slipped the ring on her finger and began replacing the books in the box.

"Look at this!" Andy cried as he reached under the desk and pulled out a large, black object that appeared to be a lump of coal. It was very shiny, as if it had been lacquered to keep the blackness from rubbing off. "I guess it was used as a paperweight or something."

"Maybe that was the first piece of coal taken from the mine," April said. She had picked up all the books, but Andy still stared at the coal. "Drop it in the box and let's get out of here."

"This thing seems to have a crack in it," he said, turning it over slowly.

"Probably broke when it fell," April replied, impatient to leave now that her ring had been found. But Andy continued to study the lump.

"When the light hits it a certain way, I can see something yellow in the crack."

211

April looked at him and sighed. "I've heard that lack of sleep makes people see things. If we hang around here any longer, we'll both be seeing purple alligators. Let's go!"

"Look for yourself," Andy urged. "Hold this in the lamplight and see if there isn't something in that crack."

Reluctantly she took the chunk of coal and revolved it. There *was* a trace of yellow in the crack!

"Must be another kind of rock inside," she said as Andy took the lump again. He picked up one of the spoons Raffles had stolen and inserted the handle into the crack, working it gingerly back and forth. The crack grew larger.

"There's a line all the way around this thing, like it's supposed to come apart." He moved the spoon along the line, and the opening spread. Then, quite suddenly, the lump separated in half; and a shower of gold coins rained out. Andy stood openmouthed, holding a piece of the coal in each hand.

"How about that!" he kept repeating.

April stared. Little sleep and the events of the evening before had left her mind too numb to accept any more surprises. "I just know I'm going to wake up any minute and find this is a dream. And it's a shame, too, because it's such a lovely dream."

Andy scooped up a handful of coins. "This isn't

212

any dream. These are real gold coins, and they are old. Must be very valuable by now."

"Oh, I hope so!" April cried, coming alive again with excitement. "That must be the fortune my aunts have been searching for."

"I suppose so," Andy said rather doubtfully. "But I just don't think these coins alone could account for all your grandfather's wealth—unless this was all he had left."

April picked up one of the halves of coal and examined it. "That was clever, hollowing it out like that. I'll bet he did use this as a paperweight, and no one ever suspected what was in it."

Andy picked up the other half. "They fit together so perfectly, it's almost impossible to tell it isn't a solid lump of coal." He glanced into the hollow, then quickly looked into it again.

"Hey! There's something stuck in this half!" He pulled out a folded paper.

April knelt beside him on the chilly floor as he carefully opened the yellowed sheet and spread it under the lamp. They looked at it closely, straining to read the unintelligible markings it contained.

"I can't make heads or tails of it," April complained.

Andy studied the paper from every angle. "These lines that look like scratches must be drawings," he muttered.

April looked at the paper again. The longer she stared at it, the more familiar the lines appeared. "I think they're supposed to represent stones—and that could be a window."

They both looked up at the wall of the tower and the tiny windows above. "I believe you're right!" Andy said slowly. "And look!" He pointed to the handwriting below the crude drawing. "If that's *e.w.*—and I think it is—that could mean east wing, maybe this very wall."

"But there are two towers in the east wing. Which could it be?"

They studied the paper once more. "That thing beside the window is probably the key," Andy said. "What do you suppose it is?"

"I don't know. Looks like a scary face, maybe a mask. But that wouldn't help much."

They looked at each other blankly. "I hope this whole thing isn't some kind of joke," April said. "My grandfather may have had an odd sense of humor."

"I don't think so," Andy told her. "I think he made the drawing for his own benefit when he realized his memory was failing—then forgot where he'd hidden this reminder."

"Well, he certainly was no artist! I wish he'd made this weird-looking thing a little clearer. It still looks like a mask to me."

214

Andy became excited. "Maybe it *is* a mask! A primitive one, like a medicine man's mask. Maybe it's a symbol for *savage.*"

"Savage?" she repeated dully, then laughed in delight. "The Savage tower! Oh, Andy! You're a genius!"

"I thought you'd never notice," he joked. "But you'd better hold the applause until we check this out. We can start from here because this is the Savage tower. There's the *S* chiseled on the wall over there."

"Oh, I'm sure this is right!" April cried. "And this scribbling down here on the paper must tell which part of the wall to search."

They pored over the mixture of letters and numbers beneath the sketch.

"That looks like *3d-4r,*" Andy deciphered. "Maybe it means three down and four right—not very complicated, but if the old gentleman wrote this for himself, there was no need to make it like a treasure map."

April said, "There's a line through the middle of the window, so maybe you start counting from the center there and count down three rows of stones and then four stones to the right."

Andy looked up at the windows around the top of the tower.

"Now the question is, which window. It isn't

likely there would be something hidden below every one."

April pointed to the sheet. "What about that cross near the edge there? That looks like the points of the compass. See, there's an $N$ at the top of the vertical line. If we hold the paper with that line facing north, then it would mean that window."

They turned toward the probable window, and Andy examined the wall. "There's only one way to find out," he said.

Gathering up a hammer and chisel the women had left, he set to work loosening the mortar around the stone the drawing seemed to indicate. After a few blows, he put down his tools.

"That's odd! There's mortar around this stone, but it's not really cemented to the wall. It just looks that way."

Using both hands, he tugged at the stone until he had worked it from its slot and placed it on the floor. April held her breath while he reached into the hole where the stone had rested. He pulled back his hand—and there was nothing in it.

April's expectations were shattered. She had been so sure they were on the right trail. Then Andy stood with his side pressed hard against the wall and stuck his arm far back into the opening. When he withdrew it this time, he clutched a small, metal box.

216

They flopped on the cold floor while he pried off the rusty lock. April tried to keep her imagination in check, but visions of gold and jewels loomed before her. When the lock had yielded, Andy handed her the box.

"You open it," he said.

Slowly she raised the lid. A moldy envelope lay on top; the dampness had invaded even this metal container. She picked up the envelope and looked inside. It held a thick sheaf of paper money—the top bill had "1000" printed in the corner—more money than she had ever seen!

April silently handed Andy the envelope while she checked the rest of the contents of the box. There were no jewels, only stocks or bonds of some kind.

Andy riffled the stack of bills and whistled. "This ought to pay the taxes for a while! There's enough . . ."

"Look!" April interrupted. "Here's another paper with drawings just like the other one. This one has *w.w.* on it. You don't suppose there's something hidden in the west wing, too?"

Andy took the paper and studied it as April replaced the items in the box.

"I'm sure these are directions for locating something hidden in the other wing," Andy said. "And it should be a little easier to find. See, that's a crude sketch, but you can tell it's a man's jacket."

"You're ahead of me again," April told him. "What's a jacket . . . Oh! Tweed! The Tweed tower!"

"That's my guess," Andy said.

"It's fantastic!" April whispered. Without warning, all the dammed up tension and excitement of the last twenty-four hours broke right over her head and swept her helplessly along. She put her head on her knees and began to laugh and cry at the same time.

"For Pete's sake, April! What's wrong?" Andy asked in alarm. "Everything's working out fine!"

"I know!" she finally managed to sob. "I can't help it. I'm so happy!"

Andy sighed. "Well, you could have fooled me." He dug into his pocket for his handkerchief and pressed it in her hand. "Here! Dry your eyes," he said gently. "Women scare me when they cry."

"I'm sorry," she sniffed. "It's just that all this money and everything has made me sort of rattled." She wiped her eyes and blew her nose. "Won't Mrs. MacDonald be furious?" The thought brought a smile to her face. "Can you believe I thought this was going to be a dull place to live? You never can tell how things are going to turn out, can you?"

Andy looked at her for a long moment. "No, you never can tell," he said. He began scooping up the gold coins and placing them in the hollow coal. "Your aunts will enjoy opening this up again."

As April watched, some of the coins slipped through his fingers. It reminded her of something.

"That's it!" she cried so suddenly that Andy dropped the coins.

"What's it?" he asked, looking startled.

"It's just like the fortune-teller told me. I'd meet a dark stranger, and he'd have gold dripping from his hands. And there you are, your fingers full of gold coins!"

This stranger had changed her life, too. But she couldn't tell him that—not yet.

Andy finished picking up the coins and stood up, then held out his hand and helped her to her feet.

"Your fortune-teller was wrong," he said and grinned at her puzzled look.

"I may have dark hair, but I'm not a stranger. I'm your friend."

April smiled up at him. "Yes, you are my friend," she said softly.